MW01128626

THE ELVIS ENIGMA

A VEGAN VAMP MYSTERY

CATE LAWLEY

Copyright © 2016 Catherine G. Cobb
All rights reserved.

ALSO BY CATE LAWLEY

VEGAN VAMP

Adventures of a Vegan Vamp

The Client's Conundrum

The Elvis Enigma

The Nefarious Necklace

DEATH RETIRED

Death Retires

THE GOODE WITCH MATCHMAKER

Timely Love

Ghostly Love

Deathly Love

Forgotten Love

The Goode Witch Matchmaker Collection

Writing as Kate Baray

LOST LIBRARY

Lost Library

Spirited Legacy

Defensive Magic

Lost Library Collection: Books 1-3

Witch's Diary

Lost Library Shorts Collection

The Covered Mirror: A Lost Library Halloween Short

Krampus Gone Wild: A Lost Library Christmas Short

SPIRELLI PARANORMAL INVESTIGATIONS

Spirelli Paranormal Investigations Season 1

Entombed: A Spirelli Investigations Novel

Writing as K.D. Baray

BEAUREGARD

Mistaken: A Seth Beauregard Short

BONUS CONTENT

Sign up for my newsletter to receive release announcements, bonus materials, and a sampling of my different series. Sign up at http://eepurl.com/b9IH5v

1

PO-PO AND THE POKEY

W hy were the police parked in front of my house?

Alex and I had just finished up a case, and neither of us was in a state of mind to be questioned. My best guess as I pulled into my driveway and parked was that Detective Ruiz was back with more questions about my murdered neighbor, Mrs. A. He'd been by a few days ago to ask several seemingly innocuous, you're-only-a-witness-type questions. So far as the police knew, she'd died under suspicious circumstances. And as a part of the investigation into her death, Detective Ruiz had interviewed the condo residents who'd known her—including me.

Little did Detective Ruiz know exactly *how* suspicious Mrs. A's death had been. The person responsible for killing Mrs. A was a vampire. A very dead, very executed vampire. Except I couldn't tell Detective Ruiz that, because vamps and wizards and all the other enhanced beings running around Austin weren't "out."

But at least my progenitor—the serial-killer bad guy who'd offed Mrs. A and turned me all vampy—had been caught. While the Society for the Study of Occult and Paranormal Phenomena had a less-than-modern justice system, it was the lone governing body for enhanced beings. And the sentence for the willy-nilly turning of humans into vamps and—this was the important bit—letting them roam free with no training or preparation was hanging.

My progenitor hadn't intended to turn me or the one other survivor. No, Gladys and I had been accidents. Neither of us had a natural immunity to the vampire virus, so—oops—baby vampires. The rest of his victims had died. It turned out that most humans were immune to the virus in small doses, but had an allergic response to it in large quantities. Not that killing several humans had been a crime in the eyes of the Society—just the carelessness with which it was done. Ugh, my head was starting to hurt.

"Hey, you okay?" Alex asked.

I picked my head up off the steering wheel. I didn't even remember resting my forehead on it. "I really am too tired to deal with the dishy Detective Ruiz."

"Give the guy a break; he's not a sex object."

I tipped my head to examine Alex—speaking of sex objects. "Yeah. So, are you going to put a shirt on, or what?"

Alex cursed. He was usually careful not to allow anyone to see the tattoos covering his torso. Probably because they were all about dark magic, bad spirit things, and represented what I'd come to realize were shameful choices from his past. But that's how tired *he* was: he'd forgotten about losing his shirt earlier in our showdown with a big, bad killer.

Sleuthing was rough stuff.

"I'll go around back and come in through Wembley's room, grab a shirt, and meet you in the kitchen."

I rubbed my temple. "Sold." I started to get out of the car

then stopped and said, "Not the Hawaiian shirt." My vamp roomie Wembley loved that shirt.

Alex gave me a disdainful look. "Please."

"Yeah, not sure what I was thinking." But I was talking to myself, because Alex had already left.

I took a breath to calm my nerves and then got out of the car. The dishy detective awaited.

But Detective Ruiz wasn't the only one waiting for me when I walked in the house. Two uniformed police officers accompanied him, and Wembley was hovering. My roomie was an ex-Viking berserker—many years removed and now very retired from pillaging and violence in general—but he still wasn't the type to hover.

I had a moment of panic, because finding the police in my house was scary. But there was no reason to panic; I was a law-abiding citizen.

Then I realized that wasn't *exactly* true. I might have murdered someone.

Definitely killed—but only maybe murdered. Murder implied a dead *human* person, and the person I'd killed hadn't been entirely of the human persuasion. I knew I was covered under the Society's laws, because it had been a just execution—or maybe self-defense? I was a little fuzzy on the details if not the outcome. The police, on the other hand, were another story.

I tried to do a casual examination of my clothing, because I'd smelled a faint odor of blood in the car as I'd driven home. My brief inspection didn't reveal anything that jumped out and said, "blood spatter!" So whatever stink had assaulted my nose in the car, the source shouldn't be noticeable to the three mundane cops in the room.

I smiled at the detective.

He looked back with a blank expression. "Mallory Andrews, I have a warrant for your arrest."

My smile faded. No way they'd found that dead body—technically two dead bodies—and gotten a warrant so quickly. My brain flitted over possibilities: illegal vampirism? I had never even bitten anyone...and that was also insane. So I sucked it up and asked, "I'm sorry—what for?"

And as I asked the question, several much more realistic possibilities skittered through my brain. If not the two dead bodies from today, then maybe the dead guy that had been in Gladys's herb garden. Although that corpse had been dug up and disposed of. Then maybe Celia, a recently murdered djinni. But I'd never even been near Celia, and I was certain her remains were equally in the wind.

I could feel panic swelling. How were there so many dead bodies in my recent past?

Maybe I was wrong and it wasn't too soon for the two casualties from today to be found. Was I getting picked up for the execution I'd committed less than an hour or two ago? The Society should have handled the corpses...but I couldn't be sure.

Finally, Detective Ruiz said, "On suspicion of murder."

Forget that the rat detective had been watching my reaction as I'd agonized over why I was being arrested. I had bigger problems than Detective Ruiz's invasive scrutiny. Reality crashed in on me. Murder? I was in serious trouble.

I wet my lips then said, "What?" I tried to rein in the panic but failed, and it seeped into my voice.

Panic, confusion, dismay; it was splashing around in my head. I'd gone through the list of recently dead people. Not only did I not murder any of them—minus the evil lady who would have been hung by the Society, so she didn't count—but the cops shouldn't know any of them were dead.

"Who?" Alex asked in a calm voice.

I did a double take. I hadn't even seen him join us in the hallway. No Hawaiian shirt, so that was a bonus. I stifled a hysterical giggle at the inappropriate thought. Then I noticed that the navy T-shirt he'd donned covered all of his tattoos. Of course it did.

"Elizabeth Ann Smith." Detective Ruiz's voice startled me, and I turned back to see he held a pair of cuffs in his hands.

I could only stare. Liz? My coworker. My very human coworker. The police thought I had killed a woman who'd been another of my progenitor's victims. I almost did laugh then. But I cut the sound short after only a small gasp escaped.

Still, I couldn't believe... "Liz? You think I killed Liz?" I looked from the stern features of Detective Ruiz to Alex and Wembley.

"Not a word." Alex didn't move a muscle. He looked relaxed and calm, not even a little worried about me being carted off by the police. For murder.

Or he wasn't calm—just that tired. The guy had been possessed a few hours ago. That thought grounded me and erased all remnants of hysteria.

I turned to Ruiz, narrowed my eyes, and said with the clearest enunciation I could manage, "You have lost your mind."

Detective Ruiz's left eye twitched. I filed that away for future reference, because something about this situation disturbed the detective deeply. It was all there in the eye twitch. I might not know what, but it was a good sign *some-*

thing hinky was afoot. I held my hands out in front of me and waited for the detective to slip his cuffs on my wrists.

As I walked to his cruiser, he read me my rights. And that was when laughter burbled again in my throat. This time, it wasn't hysteria, simply displaced and completely inappropriate amusement. Because I was a vampire, and I was pretty darn sure there was a solid legal argument that Miranda didn't apply to me. Not human, not a person; that about summed it up.

I was so screwed.

"Not a word, Mallory," Alex said again as he followed us outside. "We'll send your attorney to meet you at the station."

As I climbed into the back of the cruiser, I couldn't help thinking: *I have an attorney? Who could that possibly be?*

2

ELVIS IS IN THE BUILDING

"**F**or an Elvis impersonator, you don't actually look much like Elvis." Elvis and I were waiting to be booked, and I couldn't resist mentioning the obvious.

A deep chuckle was the man's response. "Funny thing that, because"—he leaned in close—"I'm the real deal. Or close enough." Then he settled back in his seat.

The real deal? What did that mean? Was this guy claiming to be the real Elvis?

I scooted over in my chair to get a better look. No. No way. Crazy. Because... Elvis was dead.

Yeah, the irony of that hit me about half a second later, given my own less-than-fully-alive state. Dead, undead, living but not aging. I struggled with the question of my own "aliveness"—at least I did when I cared to think about it. I'd been a little busy since I'd become a vamp.

I lifted my cuffed hands. "My first time. You?"

"Oh, no. It's part of the gig. Drugs, alcohol, disturbing the peace." He sat in his chair looking nothing like an alcoholic, drug-abusing, peace-disturbing Elvis. And I didn't even know if the original had done all those things. I wasn't exactly an expert.

The man was fit and had an even tan; he practically glowed with sobriety and health. I'd be much more likely to believe he'd stepped off a tennis court than recently been breaking the law. Well, except that his white, sparkly seventies suit wouldn't work on the courts.

I felt it might be rude to point this out, so I asked, "What are you in for this time?"

"Unpaid traffic ticket."

I choked on a laugh. But then he grinned, and I couldn't stop myself; I just let it fly. When I'd gotten my chuckles under control, I said, "How did you let you that happen?"

"It's complicated. I had to leave town in a rush, and larger concerns kept me busy." He spread his hands wide. "I forgot."

As a recently turned vamp, I did indeed know how it was to have one's priorities upended. "Wow. That really sucks. I'm sorry."

He shrugged like it wasn't a problem. Then he gave me a slow, lazy smile—and there was just a hint of Elvis. The smile broadened and that hint became so much more.

"Yeah." I nodded in wonder. "Yeah, now I see it. That smile is one hundred percent Elvis. Wow. How do you do that?"

"You do you; I'll do me." He winked. "You should check out my show. The music's not bad." But he said it like he knew exactly how fabulous the music was.

A broad grin stretched across my face. "Sure thing."

He gave me the name of a local venue just as Detective Ruiz was finishing whatever paperwork had tied him up.

"If you're done socializing?" The detective hadn't relaxed an inch since he'd put the cuffs on me, and that had the unexpected result of making me much more comfortable.

Detective Ruiz's dress was blown up over something, and while I had no idea what that could be, it meant that whatever he had against me was far from a sure thing. The confidence just wasn't there.

Waving a final farewell to Elvis—either the real deal or close enough—I stood up, not anywhere near ready to find out how much trouble I was in.

I walked in front of the detective with his hand on my upper arm, guiding me forward. "Where are we headed?"

"To an interview room." Not really chitchatty, the detective.

Once he'd situated me in the interview room, he left. That was when I remembered. I had an attorney—whoever that was—so they couldn't question me until that mysterious person arrived.

Another thirty minutes passed. I just sat in the room, by myself, and twiddled my thumbs.

Until Cornelius walked in. Formerly COO of the Society, Cornelius was acting CEO. (The previous CEO had been murdered and buried in a client's herb garden for a little while.) Cornelius was, for all intents and purposes, the mayor of the enhanced community in Austin.

I was surprised by how happy I was to see the old guy, especially since he could be a tricky dude to deal with. "Hey, Cornelius..."

A petite blonde woman followed him into the interview room. Star—heck, I didn't even know her last name. Cute features, beautiful skin, and pale blonde hair, she hardly looked the part of a witch—though she was the only one I'd met.

"You're my attorney?" I asked her. Because the last time

I'd talked to her—only days before—she'd been a mortician.

She held up a finger then turned and briskly walked the perimeter of the room. No nonsense, just like the last time we'd met. If I had to guess, I'd say she was doing the witchy version of sweeping for listening devices.

When she returned, she stopped a few feet from Cornelius and me and closed her eyes. She took one deep breath through her nose and then exhaled through her mouth. She opened her eyes and said, "Go. You've got fifteen minutes, maybe a little more."

"The room has been sealed." Cornelius motioned to a seat at the table. "We can speak freely."

I sat down, my gaze flipping between Star and Cornelius. Star had picked up a chair, moved it to a corner, and was typing on her phone—clearly not my attorney.

Cornelius seated himself opposite me. Oh my. "*You're* my attorney? Is that even legal? Don't you have to be licensed to represent me?"

His lips twitched. "I am licensed. I even went to law school in Texas."

I narrowed my eyes. "Uh-huh. When?"

"The mid-1800s."

I covered my face with my hands then spread my fingers and peeked at Cornelius. "I'm going to prison."

Apparently, this was all a big joke to him, because he had a distinctly twinkly look around his eyes. "You're not going to prison. You won't even make it to jail." He winked at me. "I'll even wager that you'll walk out with me."

Right. I could feel my heart racing in my chest. Whatever Alex said was normal for vamps, I could still hyperventilate and have panic attacks. "Is there anyone else? Maybe someone who has been licensed in *this* century?"

Cornelius just waved his hand dismissively. "I'm currently licensed. Listen—have you been booked?"

I bit my lip. Had I? "What exactly does that involve?"

"Fingerprints, pictures, official forms..."

"No, although they took my phone, made me empty my pockets, that type of thing." I normally considered Cornelius a very competent person—in his world. But this was the world of cops and jail time, not magic and vampire viruses.

"I have an inside source with the police. They don't have any solid evidence against you. Certainly nothing that the current DA would consider sufficient to bring to trial."

"Oh. My. God." I wanted to smack him. "Could you not have started with that?"

Underground sources I could totally buy into. Information acquired through bribery, coercion, magical persuasion —all things that, while troubling, I believed Cornelius had mastered long ago. Staying current with the law...that was another matter altogether.

"Why is Star here? I thought she was retired." Midnight magical autopsies didn't really say *retired*, and that was what she'd been doing when I met her, but "retired" was her official story.

She was still quietly tapping away on her phone in the corner, but when I said her name she looked up. "Semi-retired. And I'm here because I'm the only witch in the area who can seal a room without suspicious paraphernalia."

I grinned. "Thank you." Although I was sure she appreciated the wad of cash she was earning for her four kids' college funds more than my thanks.

She raised her pale eyebrows. "Police stations and magic paraphernalia do not mix well. And you're welcome."

As for the trappings of the witch trade, I couldn't even

CATE LAWLEY

begin to guess what magic paraphernalia might be. Toad tongues and wombat poop? Or more along the lines of ritual daggers and blood? My lip curled at the thought of blood.

I opted against asking, because I wasn't sure my stomach was up to the answer. But I did have other questions. For one, how long I'd be here, since I would rather not have my fangs descend if I went too long without food. Awkward.

I leveled Cornelius with a stare. "What exactly is the plan?"

"Simple enough. You keep your mouth completely shut and let me pry out of this Detective Ruiz what exactly it is that he's trying to accomplish with your arrest."

"He thinks I know something. And I do—I know who killed Liz. Or do you think they found forensics linking me to the house?"

"No. I'd know if they did." Cornelius turned to the door; a second later there was a knock, and the door opened.

Cornelius was classified as an assassin, an enhanced being with great stealth, strength, and, I was pretty sure, laser-beam eyes. I added super-hearing to the list.

Detective Ruiz entered the room alone. At least he'd ditched his backup. I was hardly a threat. Although I did have a magical sword who came when called—so maybe I was *little* dangerous. The thought made me smile.

And then I met Detective Ruiz's unamused gaze. I wiped the smile off my face.

"I have neither the time nor the inclination to sit in this room for any significant length of time." Cornelius's British accent leaked more than usual as he bit out the words. "We are both aware that my client did not murder Elizabeth Smith. That they were merely coworkers."

Cornelius motioned for Star to join us.

Detective Ruiz waited for her to sit down, then said, "Your client knew Liz was dead before the police had processed the scene. She interviewed a coworker, asking specific questions that made it clear she was aware of Elizabeth's death long before the information was publicly available. She knows something—maybe the identity of the murderer."

"So you arrested my client without cause."

"I had a warrant." Detective Ruiz was looking remarkably unflustered. If I had to guess, I'd say the guy thrived on conflict, because he looked a lot more at ease dealing with a contentious Cornelius than he had with me earlier. Eventually, he added, "But she's free to go at any time. And I apologize for any inconvenience."

I was about to stand up and exit the station with near-vamp speed—because free!—when Cornelius put his hand on my forearm.

I gritted my teeth, then settled back into my seat. And, remembering his instructions, didn't say a word.

"Tell us what you want, so that Ms. Andrews isn't required to suffer the indignity of a second, equally unsubstantiated arrest."

I noticed he didn't say illegal. So there must have been some evidence presented to the judge issuing the warrant.

"I think she knows who killed her friend Liz. And Amelia Baker. And Violet Smith, Maria Sanchez, Gloria Steck, and six other women."

Uh-oh. I recognized those names as my progenitor's other victims. Deaths that should have looked like an allergic reaction, not murder. I glanced at Cornelius, but his expression of professional uber-calm hadn't flickered.

"I'm not certain what information you think Ms. Andrews has, but I'm sure you're mistaken." Cornelius turned to me and asked, "Do you have information relevant to the detective's investigation?"

I shook my head—and didn't open my mouth. I was downright proud of myself.

Detective Ruiz pointed a finger at me. "Your client has a terrible poker face. She recognized the names."

And that little bit of pride I'd felt for my silence deflated with what sounded suspiciously in my mind like a fart and then fluttered away.

Turning to me, Detective Ruiz said, "You need to tell me what you know about those women's deaths. No way eleven women of similar age and profession all located within a small geographic region and possessing no known allergies all die of anaphylactic shock."

Oh, how right he was. But I still didn't say anything.

My silence frustrated him far more than his interaction with Cornelius. Or maybe he was just mad that he'd over-shared. Now we knew why he was chasing the cases.

"We're done." Cornelius stood up. "I'll have a look at the supposed evidence you provided for the warrant. And if there's anything out of order, you can expect a complaint to be filed. If you contact my client again, expect a complaint to be filed. If you even hint that she's committed an unlawful act without the appropriate evidence to support your claims, a complaint will be filed."

I felt a little bad for Detective Ruiz. The guy was only doing what I'd been trying to do a few weeks ago: get justice for the women my progenitor had harmed. That he'd even discovered that the deaths weren't natural was amazing, and worthy of some respect.

The detective didn't look concerned by Cornelius's threats. He looked angry. Then again, he was pretty sure I knew the identity of a murderer who'd killed at least eleven women and was keeping mum. That would make me angry, too.

I stood up and followed Cornelius and Star out of the interview room. Once we'd cleared the doorway, I asked, "Can I speak now?"

"No." Cornelius didn't say anything else to me until we'd retrieved my personal effects and exited the station. "Alex is waiting around the corner for you."

That wasn't good, not at all. He'd been possessed by a demon only hours ago. "He should be getting some rest."

"We would *all* rather be doing other things." Cornelius gave me that look, the one where I felt like a scolded schoolgirl.

The man was annoying. It wasn't my fault that I'd been snatched up by the police, so how he managed to make me feel bad about it... I really was tempted to blow a raspberry at the man. I refrained.

With a hard look, Cornelius said, "Do not speak to Detective Ruiz. The man has latched on to the case with an obsessive passion that will undoubtedly cause us some difficulty—and I don't need you making it worse."

I shrugged and widened my eyes innocently. "Who, me?"

A tiny glint of silver peeked out from his eyes.

I narrowed my eyes. "That won't work. Alex told me you do that on purpose."

"Usually. I usually do it on purpose. You, Ms. Andrews, bring out the worst in me."

There wasn't really an appropriate response to that, so I gave him a little wave and hotfooted it around the corner. Then I remembered Star. I turned back and called out, "Thank you."

And I'd swear she winked at me.

I might develop a liking for that woman. She was pretty cool, even if she did deal with creepy dead bodies all day long.

"Mallory," Alex called out from my right.

I looked around and spotted him parked at the curb in his Nissan Juke.

I waved and headed across the street. Once I'd hopped in the car, I said, "Thanks for picking me up—although you should have gone home and gotten some sleep."

He raised an eyebrow. "And leave you to the mercies of the mundane policing force? Are you sure about that?"

That was an unpleasant thought, since I was already getting hungry.

Without a word, Alex handed me a spicy veggie juice. The man was always prepared. I did adore that about him.

I drank about half the small bottle in one long pull. "Thank you. Hey, you won't believe who I met. How do you feel about going with me to see an Elvis impersonator?"

3

DITHERING OVER DATES

"Elvis?" Alex pulled out into traffic. "Why Elvis? Oh—and is this a date?"

"Huh?" I mentally stuttered over the word *date*. Considered answering, then decided that was a bad, bad idea. "I was thinking you could check to see if the guy has some kind of magic. He said he was Elvis. The real Elvis. Sort of."

"Possible. Although I thought he left the area a while ago."

"I'm sorry—are you saying that Elvis lives in Austin?"

"Lived, and he's not exactly Elvis. No clue where he is now. And you shouldn't be able to recognize him."

"Are you telling me that the real Elvis is alive, has had work done to not look like Elvis, and now works as an Elvis impersonator. So he's the real guy playing at being someone else who plays at being himself?" My brain was going to explode.

Alex shrugged. "Not exactly. Ask Wembley. He's a fan."

"Why is that not weird to you?"

"If you mean the Elvis thing, well, he probably thinks it's

funny. I understand the guy has an odd sense of humor. But if you mean Wembley being a fan... The transformation crosses wires in most of you guys' brains, and it's not usually an improvement—you and Wembley being the exception, of course. But it's possible obsessive fandom might be a side effect in Wembley's case."

"Ha! I knew it. I knew there was something specific about vamps you didn't you like. Why wouldn't you tell me that before?" I'd been asking him ever since we met why he didn't like vampires.

"What am I supposed to say? Your brain is wired weirdly? What good would that do? And you seem fine—unlike most vamps." He was getting on the freeway, so all of his attention was on merging. He was convinced the world was filled with terrible drivers—me included. He wasn't far off, given that most of us didn't have the speed and agility of a wizard.

Crossed wires did answer one glaring question.

"That does make Gladys's particular quirks a little more understandable." To say that Gladys had unique ways of thinking was an understatement.

Alex tipped his head and his lips quirked. "She marches to the beat of her own drum. I wonder if she came up with the Divorced Divas club before or after the transformation."

"Oh, that was before. But about seeing Elvis, or the almost Elvis?"

He grinned. "Let's go and check it out."

"It's a date." I was so excited that I spat out the first thing that came to mind. The idea of meeting Elvis would do that to a girl.

And then I rode in awkward silence for five more minutes because I had to dissect what exactly that meant. Was it a *date* date? Or an appointment date? Alex had acted like a proprietary jerk when Detective Ruiz had first interviewed me a few days ago. He'd kissed me on the cheek so he could whisper something in my ear unobtrusively—so that didn't really count as any real interest. Then again, he had dated or slept with what seemed to be a large percentage of the women in the Society. Not that I'd met many, but—

"Hey. We're here," Alex said.

I blushed. Which was silly, because there was no way that he knew I'd been obsessing over our Elvis outing for the last several minutes.

"You and the blushing." He shook his head. "On the off chance the world doesn't already know you as the blushing vampire, I would try to get a handle on that when you're in mixed company. You want to keep your strengths and weaknesses close when you're dealing with the enhanced community."

"Seriously? What's the big deal? Are you telling me that you've never seen a vampire blush?"

"Most don't seem to care enough. And those who do, like Wembley, are old and long past blushing."

"Huh." I really couldn't see how a physical response to discomfort could be eradicated from an entire class of enhanced beings. And I had a hard time seeing myself as so completely *other*. I mean, how much more "other" could I get? I was a freaking vampire. Now I was supposed to be some kind of subcategory of vamp? "What about the tears?"

He looked uncomfortable with the question. "I had Star look into it." He glanced at me.

Then I realized what his issue was. "You think I'm pissed that you told someone? Someone you trust, while trying to help me. Really, it's okay. Now tell me what the heck is going on with the garlic I leak from my eyes."

"First, it's not garlic, it just smells like garlic. When I described it, Star thought it sounded like a potion that some witches manufacture called bitter tears. It's—ah—it's corrosive to vampires."

My eyeballs were bugging out. I knew because they started to itch, and I realized I wasn't blinking.

He ran a hand through his hair. "This is why we haven't had this conversation. You okay?"

"Not really. You're saying I cry some kind of witch's brew that acts as vampire repellent from my vampire eyes. That's nuts."

"Potion," he said. I turned to look at him, and Alex shrugged. "Bitter tears is the name of a potion, meaning that it's brewed from several ingredients. Brewing is the act of combining different ingredients through magical means— as well as mechanical and chemical—to create a potion."

"Great. Now I need an alchemy lesson to understand my bodily functions."

"Actually, alchemy is a totally different— Ah, right, not important. The point is: you're not crying a witch's potion. The reverse, in fact. The potion was made to mimic vampire tears. That stuff leaking out of your eyes is highly toxic to witches."

"I cry tears that are toxic to witches, and witches brew some kind of potion that's similar—"

"But altered in a significant and fundamental way to target vampires."

I laughed as a stray thought planted itself in my brain. "I can't even begin to imagine how much this information cost. I don't see Star parting with this for anything less than extortionate amounts. Oh!" I bounced in the passenger seat. "You just proved that I'm not the only the vamp that cries! Ha—so there."

He shot me a crooked smile. "Glad that's your takeaway."

I stopped bouncing. "Wait, what's yours?"

"That not many vamps cry, or I would have known all this already—and saved myself a small fortune—and that you should aerosolize your tears. Sounds like a wicked weapon in a pinch." He raised his eyebrows. "One that doesn't require any particular training."

"Hey, I'm working on that. Tangwystl and my lessons are going very well, thank you." I got out of the car. "But just in case, how toxic are we talking? Injured, maimed, or dead?" A trial run seemed like a bad idea without at least that little tidbit of information.

"Not deadly." He grinned then leaned across the passenger seat so he could meet my gaze. "So experiment away."

Was I that transparent?

"Oh, what about Elvis? Hang on." I pulled out my phone and looked up Tiaras, the venue Elvis had given me. Oddly, it was in South Austin rather than downtown. Not what I expected for an Elvis show. I flipped to the events page. "Three more nights, nine to eleven. When do you want to go?"

"Why not tonight? Plenty of time to catch up on sleep before then. I'll pick you up around eight. And tell Wembley. He won't care if the guy's an Elvis imposter or impersonator."

'kay. Not a *date* date if Wembley was coming along. "Exactly how much of a fan is Wembley?"

Alex grinned. "Hardcore."

Wembley. And Elvis. Wembley crushing over a retro popstar. It was too delicious for words.

"See you at eight." I shut the door without waiting for a

response and hurried into the house—because I had to see this right now.

Forget that I was an oddly teary vamp.

Or that my evening outing with Alex was so clearly not a romantic date.

I was ready to be entertained be an ancient Viking vamp going all fanboy crazy.

And I wasn't disappointed. Five minutes later, my eyes were bulging and my cheeks were sore from holding back a smile.

Elvis's name had barely passed my lips when Wembley disappeared into his bedroom to retrieve "something special."

It was special, all right. Special in a glitzy, glam, Elvis-impersonator suit kind of way.

"It's nice. Is it accurate?" I looked at the white rhine-stone-studded suit Wembley had pulled out of a garment bag. "I mean, is it from the period?"

Wembley ran his hand down the white fabric. "I had it designed from several photos I took at one of his concerts."

"And you carry your Elvis suit with you every time you move?" As a house flipper, Wembley had been moving into his almost completed projects to orchestrate the final remodel details for ages.

"Of course not. I'm not a nut. Halloween's just around the corner, so I pulled it out of storage. That's really the only time I can wear it anymore."

Versus a few years ago when he could wear it walking down the street in Austin? A little giggle escaped.

"Laugh all you want. I'm used to it. But Elvis is the man. He's totally worth any flack I get."

"So I guess that's a yes to this evening's outing."

Wembley looked at me like I'd lost it. "I wouldn't miss it. I'm surprised I didn't know he was performing locally."

"You do understand that it might not be the actual Elvis. Probably isn't the actual Elvis. I mean, this guy really didn't look anything like *the* Elvis."

"He wouldn't, would he? He's had work done. A few times, I think. Or maybe he can change his own appearance? I'm not really sure."

My face contorted as I tried to work out how exactly a surgeon would slice and dice *the* Elvis to come up with *my* Elvis. And failing that, how a guy could change his own face. "But can they change that much about a person's face?"

"If 'they' are utilizing magic to make the alterations, then sure."

Of course there were magical plastic surgeons. Why wouldn't there be?

I shook my head. "Okay, fine. We're leaving at eight. Oh, and you are not wearing the Elvis suit."

Wembley shot me a sad puppy-dog look.

"No."

Boone, my recently acquired bloodhound, chose that moment to meander into the living room looking for food, attention, or a squishier spot to recline. He must have been asleep earlier when I'd come home.

I looked from Boone to Wembley. "You just don't have the wrinkles and puppy-dog cuteness to pull off that look. Unlike Boone." I petted the red head resting against my thigh and rubbed his silky ears.

"You're welcome for picking up your dog."

"Huh? Oh. I'm so sorry, Wembley." I forgot I'd had to leave Boone at the Society's headquarters earlier when I'd been on another case. "Thank you...but you still can't wear the Elvis suit."

"You're a hard woman, Mallory Andrews."

That was so far from the truth that I smiled. "Halloween is only a few weeks away. You can hold out, I'm sure."

Then I went to bed. My day had been much too full of dead bodies and police, and I was exhausted. Not really okay, since I might have a late night out ahead of me.

4

HECKLER HATES ON (BAD) ELVIS

L ater that night, the manager of Tiaras gave Alex and I an apologetic smile. "I'm so sorry. The show's been canceled for the evening."

I was really glad Wembley had opted to drive the three of us and was still parking.

"There's no Elvis show? It was on your website." This could not be happening. Not only would Wembley be crushed, but my crime-fighting, almost agoraphobic side-kick Bradley had agreed to leave his condo—miracle of miracles—to come with us.

Maybe Elvis hadn't been able to sort out his legal woes in time to make his evening show. But really—a traffic ticket? They couldn't still be holding the guy for that.

"And it was scheduled for this evening, but"—the manager of the venue leaned forward and lowered his voice —"we can't find him."

"Ugh. I knew I should have called ahead. He probably got stuck at the police station." I shot the manager a squinty look. "So where is he?"

"If I knew that, he wouldn't be missing." Irrefutable

logic, but irritating nonetheless. He quickly added in a conciliatory tone, "We do have a local band playing this evening instead, and I'd be glad to waive your group's cover fee."

Wembley came through the door just as the manager was offering us a free cover. "Aw, no Elvis, right? I knew it was too good to be true."

I looked at Alex, and he shrugged.

We were already here, so I went ahead and asked, "Who's playing?"

Once the manager named the band, Wembley was in. He'd seen them cover some Elvis tunes in the past. And with Wembley in, Alex and I could hardly complain. He'd driven us and he was the disappointed fan in this scenario, and, for a disappointed fan, was taking it all surprisingly well.

"Oh, we need to call Bradley." I could only imagine how upset he'd be.

Alex lifted his phone. "Already texted him." Then his phone dinged with a message. After glancing at the screen, he said, "Bradley's in."

"Wow. Really?" I was flabbergasted. Bradley was antisocial. He was a recluse, a homebody.

And he was walking through the door.

I waved. "No cover, come on in."

Wembley had already headed to the back of the place toward a door, and I'd seen that there was outdoor seating when I checked out the website early. So it looked like we were headed outside.

Bradley tucked his license back in his wallet, and I gave him a big hug. He stood there and waited for me to be done. Someday he'd learn to enjoy my awesome hugs.

"Hello." He turned to Alex. "I'd rather not shake hands."

"That's okay," Alex said. "I'm not a big fan myself."

Bradley nodded at this statement with a look of approval. Alex had probably just jumped up several pegs on the coolness chart. Which Bradley might actually have hanging up somewhere in his condo. He tended to approach human interaction a lot like a project: with a plan and goals for success.

"You know, Mrs. A would be really proud of you for getting out tonight." I gave Bradley an encouraging smile.

"I know. She said that I should mingle with people my own age who share my interests. I like Elvis's music, and you like Elvis's music—"

"Got it. I'm super proud of you."

Bradley glanced at Alex then me. "Where's the music?"

"I think out back," Alex said. "Come on. Wembley's grabbed us some seats."

Not just seats, but a table near the front. The courtyard was surprisingly thin of people. Granted, the band was just starting to set up, but as excited as Wembley and Bradley had been, I'd expected a large crowd.

I waved at Wembley to let him know we'd seen him. "Either Elvis isn't very popular or people don't come to these things early."

Bradley stopped and looked at me. "Elvis is popular."

Oops. Apparently, I'd just committed a faux pas in the land of Bradley. "Of course he is," I said. "I'm sorry."

"That's okay." But the words were grudging.

Mental note: no dissing Elvis around Bradley. Probably not Wembley either. I joined Wembley and Alex at the table and promised myself I'd be on my best behavior.

But it wasn't me who committed the next Presley faux pas. When the band started to play, I had just enough time to figure they were pretty good before a guy two tables over from us started to cause a ruckus.

At first, troublemaker guy just sang along. Not that weird; people did that. But he got louder and louder. I thought he might be drunk, but then I got a good look at him.

"Hey, Wembley. You know that guy?" I pointed, not all that discreetly, at the guy who was now singing at the top of his lungs.

Wembley didn't even look at the guy. "That's Ralph."

I raised my eyebrows. "What's Ralph's deal?"

"He heckles. Complete jerk. No respect for the King's memory." Wembley didn't even crack a smile.

I pursed my lips. "The King—who might be walking amongst us today—his memory?"

Wembley shot me a disapproving look. "That's not the point. Ralph likes to heckle anyone he thinks is subpar. He's been banned from a few venues."

First the closet Elvis fans, now a bad-Elvis heckler? "They're a cover band. It's not like they're actual Elvis impersonators. And who heckles musicians?"

"Doesn't matter who they are, just that the singing isn't up to his standards." Wembley raised his voice, shouting in Ralph's general direction. "Because Ralph's a crazy person."

The raucous, off-key singing stopped. "That you, Wembley?" Ralph stood up and started to walk toward our table. All one hundred and not very many pounds of him.

A disgruntled look crossed Wembley's face as the diminutive man approached.

I wasn't sure exactly what this small, leather-jacket-wearing elderly man hoped to accomplish, but he strode across the courtyard like he had a bone to pick with us.

When he arrived, he gave Wembley a hard look, but then turned to me and smiled. "Ralph Dukat. A pleasure to meet you…" He glanced at Wembley, clearly expecting him to complete the introduction. Wembley ignored him.

"Mallory," I said. "Nice to meet you. And this is Alex. And Bradley."

Alex and Ralph exchanged manly nods. Bradley glanced at Ralph then turned his attention back to the band. Apparently, Mrs. A's rules of polite behavior didn't extend to strange, heckling men who weren't invited.

After a brief hesitation, I said, "So—would you like to join us?"

Wembley groaned. Since I didn't have preternatural vamp hearing, that meant Ralph likely heard it, too. But Wembley's ungracious manner didn't dissuade Ralph.

He accepted with a dignified, almost stuffy tone that was at odds with his jeans and leather jacket. "Yes, thank you."

As Ralph seated himself between Alex and Wembley, Alex said, "But tone down the heckling. I don't think my ears can take your off-key singing at this distance."

Ralph cracked a grin. "I can manage that for a few minutes."

Wembley snorted in disbelief.

Ralph lifted his hands. "I come in peace." He leaned forward, looked around the table at each of us, then said in a conspiratorial stage whisper, "Wanted to see if you have any info on Elvis's disappearance."

Why he bothered to attempt any facsimile of a whisper with the band playing so near, only Ralph could know.

"Why are you asking us?" So far as this joker knew, we were just people listening to the band.

"And who says the guy's missing?" Alex sounded annoyed, but I could tell by the twitch of his lips that he was entertained by the odd, heckling interloper. Surprising, to say the least.

"Well, he's not here. So obviously he's missing." Ralph looked around the table, like we should all know this information. "Patrick never misses a show."

"Patrick?" Wembley asked, his curiosity finally outweighing his disdain.

"Yeah. Patrick Twombly." Ralph looked confused. "The guy we're here to see? Elvis?"

"Ah. I only know him as Elvis." I checked with Wembley, but he shrugged. Bradley, on the other hand...

"Whatcha got, Bradley?"

"Patrick Twombly, Elvis impersonator," Bradley said. "New to the circuit, but already making a name for himself. Recently rated as one of the best singers on the impersonation circuit."

Ralph raised his hand. "Anyone who's anyone is on the private forum where Patrick posts his appearances." He gave Wembley a superior look.

With a grumpy look on his face, Wembley said, "I'm a fan, not a crazy stalker—like some people."

I bit my lip to keep from saying I'd found the show on a very public website.

Sitting up taller in his seat and assuming a dignified expression, Ralph said, "I'm a heckler. There is a huge difference between heckling and stalking. I encourage a higher standard of performance; I do *not* stalk."

Wembley crossed his arms.

"I'm not a stalker," Bradley said. "I neither harass nor persecute, and I have not given anyone unwanted attention."

I blinked at Bradley in confusion. It took me a few seconds, but once I thought I'd translated Bradley-ese into English, I asked, "So, you're a member of this secret forum?" That was the only implication that made sense of his comment.

"Yes." He gave me that disappointed look that he reserved for moments when I'd underperformed as the ninja crime-fighting vamp he thought I was.

"He probably got hung up at the police station." The novelty of Ralph had worn off already, and Alex looked annoyed. Glancing at me, Alex said, "Most people can't circumvent the legal process with a snap of their cute, mani-cured fingers."

I glanced at my spiffy new turquoise polish, surprised he'd noticed—or thought it was cute. "Wait, what? I didn't circumvent; I'm innocent."

"Said every guilty person ever." He grunted when I elbowed him in the ribs. "It's true. It's also true that no one gets to see an attorney that fast."

"Really?"

He nodded, and the amused look was back. "Yeah."

"Wait—were you in prison with Patrick?" Ralph's eyes were about to bug out.

"Jail. I was in jail. Well, not even jail. We were in the same booking area. But he should have been able to resolve his issue quickly—it was just a traffic ticket thing."

"He was released," Bradley said. "I checked before I agreed to come tonight."

And that wasn't stalkerish. Not at all.

Ralph perked up. "You can do that?"

I pointed at Bradley and gave him a squinty look. "Not a word." Turning to Ralph, I said, "Let's assume that Bradley's information is good but not readily accessible to others." When Ralph opened his mouth, I shook my head and said, "Nope—no questions. Maybe...ah, Patrick is just sick."

Ralph didn't look very convinced of that explanation, and Wembley didn't help with his grunt of disbelief. Alex was uncharacteristically silent. And Bradley had taken my admonishment to heart; his lips were pressed tightly together.

"I'm done with you guys," I said. "You're all crazy. We're here; let's just enjoy the show. Elvis—Patrick—whatever his name is, I'm sure he's fine."

5

STALKING THE GOD OR A GOD?

Patrick Twombly was missing.

I wanted to smack myself. I deserved a day off. No, I deserved a few weeks off. But I just couldn't let it go. Bradley had been so certain Patrick had been released from police custody. And heckler-stalker Ralph was convinced Patrick wouldn't miss a show, even if he was sick—not unless he'd lost his voice, but then he'd have informed the venue manager.

So I'd gone to his house.

I really did want to smack myself now.

"Wembley!" I hollered as I walked through the front door.

"Kitchen," was his muffled response.

Just as well; I was starving. I'd grabbed a snack on my way out the door earlier this morning, but hadn't eaten since.

The smell of garlic wafted through the house. Vegan cheese soup for lunch, at a guess.

"What has you in such a tizzy?"

"I'm not in a tizzy, but I forgive you your hurtful words if you're making me cheese soup." I inhaled a deep breath, and notes of funky cheese made me smile.

"Yep. Added a little extra garlic this time, since you like your food to bite you back."

"You lovely man. When will it be done?"

"Now." He quirked an eyebrow and looked at the clock on the microwave.

I grabbed a bowl out of the cupboard. "For shame. It's never too early for cheese soup."

Once I'd settled in at the table with my steamy soup, Wembley asked, "So—where were you?"

I gave him a guilty look as I slurped vegan cheesy goo into my mouth.

He crossed his arms. "You went to Patrick's place, didn't you?"

I blinked and smiled.

"Don't flutter your eyelashes at me. I know you're not innocent. Did you go alone? Never mind, I already know the answer. How about Tangwystl?"

I swallowed and nodded eagerly. "Yes. I did bring Tangwystl."

I'd recently discovered that I could call my sword to me from across town. But I'd also discovered that was usually only possibly when a witch—a powerful witch—had bound a sword to its owner. So I pretended that particular talent wasn't one of my weird and unique not-quite-vamp enhancements, and tried to remember to carry Tangwystl whenever I might be encountering danger.

Like when I was stalking a famous dead guy.

"What did you find?"

"I didn't find Elvis. Or Patrick. Patrick-Elvis...the guy I met at the police station. Actually, there wasn't any sign of an occupant that I could see. What's that look for? I didn't break in. I swear."

Wembley sat down at the table with me. Not that he ate, but he liked to keep me company when I ate. He was sweet that way. Even if he was shooting me suspicious, accusatory looks. "And you had the right place?"

I snorted. "Bradley gave me the address. I'm sure."

"So now you're worried."

"I am." I sighed. "So do you or don't you think Patrick-Elvis is *the* Elvis?"

"Depends. If he is who I think he is, then he both is and is not Elvis. And the guy I'm thinking of recently adopted a new identity and look, so I wouldn't necessarily recognize him."

"Cryptic much?" I asked. "Never mind. If he's your guy, could he be hiding out with a debilitating flu?"

"No way. Elvis, the performer, singer, actor is dead. But there is a physical manifestation of him that runs around still, and he's highly unlikely to get sick." Wembley paused. "The guy I'm thinking of is a demigod."

"Sorry—a god?"

"Demigod."

I didn't know what to say. Because God was...God. My personal and spiritual beliefs aside, it seemed like a problem that Elvis was somehow in the same arena as God. *The* God, from the Bible.

"Stop," Wembley said.

"Huh—what?"

"Your brain's about to explode. You have that five-seconds-away-from-a-meltdown look."

"That's a specific look for me?"

Wembley shrugged.

At this point, I couldn't tell if he was trying to push my

buttons to distract me from the bigger theological question or was completely serious. "If you hadn't just made me some of the best vegan soup I'm likely ever to consume, I might be annoyed. But instead, I'm going to not be annoyed while you explain the difference between a god and a demigod and I finish my fabulous soup."

Apparently, the most important thing he heard was "fabulous soup," because a self-satisfied smirk bloomed across his face. "Easy: a mortal can become immortalized through worship—and when I say worship, think in the broadest terms possible. The process is murky, and it certainly doesn't happen often. No one seems to know why some demigods are created with a relatively small following and others with a large following, or what constitutes worship. Also, why Elvis and not Lennon?"

I didn't bite the Elvis-Lennon bait, because I was too baffled by the ramifications of his disclosure. "So, gods are walking around on earth."

"Not like you mean. Demigods are basically another form of enhanced human, just a variety that has been willed into existence by non-magical people. Demigods have magical skills and are harder to kill. They're not gods like your God." He winked. "Or my gods, for that matter. I'd place bets on Odin over Patrick any day of the week."

I chuckled. It was a little funnier and less theologically disturbing in that light. Then I remembered that there had been a reason we'd gotten onto gods versus demigods. I rested my elbows on the table. "So what do I do? Elvis—Patrick—might actually be missing. Clearly he's not sick, assuming he's the new but not necessarily improved version of Elvis."

"Why do anything? He's not your problem. Heck, I'm a fan, and I don't feel any responsibility. And there's the issue of privacy. Why poke around in the man's affairs when he hasn't asked for help? And that's always assuming he's not some innocent—and mentally incompetent—human guy that happens to think he's the real King."

I rubbed my temples. "You're right. Of course. I have no way to know if there's actually a problem, and it's certainly none of my business."

But I couldn't help feeling that maybe Patrick wasn't in a situation to ask for help.

6

AN INTREPID HOUND

Three almost blissful days passed. Sure, I occasionally thought of Patrick-Elvis. And, yes, I might have driven by his house in a stalkerish manner in hopes of seeing him entering or exiting his home—preferably all in one piece and showing no signs of ill treatment or illness. And I might have obsessively checked the Tiaras website for updates on the shows he had scheduled, all of which had been canceled.

But other than that, those three days were worry-free and wonderful. So worry-free that the tension in my shoulders and lower back had begged for a hot bath.

So here I sat in my bath, surrounded by bubbles and wondering if I'd done the right thing in walking away from the Patrick-Elvis problem. Or, if Wembley was right, and other people's lives—especially the very private lives of members of the enhanced community—were none of my business.

My phone rang, interrupting the ongoing tug-o-war inside my brain. Good thing, because after three days I didn't see that question being resolved anytime soon.

I wiped my fingers carefully on my towel, saw it was Alex, and then answered. "Hello?"

"We've got a missing kitsune." While skipping greetings wasn't odd for Alex, he wasn't typically this abrupt unless serious trouble loomed.

"A what?"

"Akira Mori has gone missing. Akira is a kitsune. A fox spirit."

I sat up so abruptly that a bubble wave splashed over the rim of the tub. "Patrick-Elvis."

"If that's your way of asking if they're linked...I don't know. I do know that Patrick Twombly is Elvis's most recently assumed identity."

The sound of a honking horn in the background gave me pause. "Are you driving?"

"I'm headed to your place. Akira's twelve-year-old daughter came home to find their house a mess and her mother absent, so this case just went to the top."

Alex coming to me for help was a big change. A nice change. I stood up, dripping bubbles.

"I need Boone to check the house for scents he might recognize and catalogue whatever he finds there."

I slipped back into the tub. "You know that Boone the wonder hound with the awesome sniffer comes with a...traveling buddy."

I almost said *partner*, but I was hardly that. His real partner, Celia, had been a djinni killed while pursuing another killer. Whatever connection she'd forged with Boone that allowed them to communicate mind to mind had done something to his little bloodhound brain. He could understand human speech and make himself understood—when I was around. No clue what part I played in the equation, only that I was a required piece.

"Right. There in five." And he hung up.

I gave my phone a nasty look. I should be more sympathetic, because Celia, Boone's dead partner, had been a friend of Alex's. But regardless of his personal feelings, I deserved an invitation. "Hey, mind coming out to the crime scene with Boone?"

I set my phone down. Yeah, that wasn't ever happening.

Five minutes later, I heard the front door open, and then, "Mallory!"

If I wasn't mistaken, that was Alex's bellowing voice. Wild guess: he'd let himself in. He could whisper just about any lock open, so the lock on the front door was no impediment.

I swallowed an annoyed grumble and headed to the entryway.

Wembley was out running errands for the morning, so wrote a quick message and pinned it to our new roomie message corkboard.

I snatched Boone's leash off its peg, hooked it to his collar, and then grabbed my keys. Finally, I turned to Alex. "I'm ready."

But he'd already opened the front door.

"We need to take mine." I threw the words over my shoulder as I sailed through the door. "I have Boone's gear in the back of my Jeep."

"All right."

I didn't bother to check, because I was certain Alex would lock up just as he'd let himself in. I clicked the key fob to unlock the car and then loaded Boone into the back.

He jumped in and settled immediately onto a huge pillow bed that took up about half of the back seat and cargo area.

Without a word, I closed the hatch and headed for the driver's seat.

"I'm sorry."

I tipped my head. "For what?" I hadn't realized I'd been so obviously peevish.

"For being so short with you on the phone."

I turned to look at him.

"I know that you and Boone are a package deal. I assumed you'd come because we needed Boone—and you're insanely nosy."

I squinted at him. Did he really think I was that petty? Then I realized I'd headed to the driver's side of the car. Maybe my nose was a little out of joint.

"I *am* insanely nosy. Not to mention there's a terrified twelve-year-old girl involved who must be missing her mom like crazy right now." I chucked the keys at him.

And I was pretty sure he mumbled, "Thank God."

As I moved around to the passenger side, I said, "You know, I'm not a terrible driver."

"You're all terrible drivers."

I snorted as I got in the passenger side of my Grand Cherokee. "Everyone who doesn't have wizard-fast reflexes, you mean."

He shrugged.

While he drove us to the scene of the crime in north central Austin, I grilled him on the details. "When was the last time anyone saw Akira?"

"She dropped her daughter Michelle off at school at seven thirty. So far as we know, that's the last time anyone saw her. She works from home and didn't have any appointments scheduled today."

"The dad?"

"Not in the picture since Michelle was a toddler. He was

mundane. I think being both married to a kitsune and having a daughter who would grow into kitsune powers was too much for him."

"You knew him?"

"I met him." Alex frowned. "Underwhelming."

Which was an interesting observation for an uninvolved man to make.

"You think highly of Akira."

He glanced at me, surprised. "Sure. Yeah, actually I do. But we didn't—"

"What? Sort of date?" I winced. "Yeah, that was really awful given the circumstances. Sorry."

"I know you think I've"—he tipped his head as he considered his words—"*dated* half of the enhanced population in Austin, but I haven't."

If dated was a euphemism for boffed them senseless... "Not really any of my business."

Wow. I was super proud of myself. The filter from my brain to my mouth was inching toward a place I could live with. Sometimes. I'd still bet on me dropping the occasional gem, if I was a betting kind of gal.

Once Alex got on the freeway, we flew down the road. Since he normally traveled with the flow of traffic, I was guessing Akira's disappearance had him worried.

After we passed a handful of cars like they were standing still, it occurred that I might feel better if I focused on the case. "Does Akira have the kind of job that would create enemies?"

"She's a financial planner, an independent." He frowned. "She does have access to private financial information. Yeah, it's possible."

"Maybe she stumbled onto something she shouldn't have seen." I texted Bradley and asked him to look at her firm. "I've got Bradley working on the big picture. Hopefully we can get her client list from her computer or physical files."

My phone dinged. I read the text and snorted. "Bradley says to get him her computer, and he'll dig up the dirt on her clients, too."

I texted: *Best sidekick ever.*

"He's handy. And not like I thought he'd be."

"Under all the awkward, Bradley's good people. Don't suppose you have some of the emergency response guys checking on Patrick-Elvis? I'm worried if he's missing that there might be a connection. Two missing people in just a few days, both members of the Society..."

"Agreed. But we'll head over there ourselves after we finish up at Akira's house. We have an ace in the hole." He glanced at Boone in the rearview mirror.

"Right! Boone can match up scents." I looked over my shoulder. "You're a rock star, Boone."

He was lying on his bed, but was wide awake. He thumped his tail. I guessed he agreed. Or maybe that was plain old regular dog language, and he was just happy to be appreciated.

"Francis and Anton responded to the call, but only Anton is on scene. Francis took Michelle to headquarters so Cornelius could question her."

"Good grief." I had visions of Cornelius's molten, mercury eyes, and how terrifying that sight could be to a kid. A freshly traumatized kid. "Please tell me Francis will stick around for the questioning."

Alex exited the freeway just north of the university and headed east. "Cornelius is good with kids. He has about ten grandkids."

"Really? Ten? Cornelius?" Alex shot an amused look my

way, and I said, "Sorry. It's just a little hard for me to see Cornelius as a grandpa."

"A doting grandpa."

"Huh. Mind-boggling." I let my mind wander down the path of a paternal Cornelius for several seconds, but I had to stop and shake off the weirdness. "So tell me about kitsune. That's what you said both Michelle and her mother Akira are. So give me the scoop on kitsune."

"Like I said, fox spirits, but I don't think Michelle actually is kitsune. At least, not yet."

"Like a were-fox." I couldn't hide my excitement. Finally, some kind of werewolf-like enhanced being. It was about time.

"No, like a kitsune. What is your hang-up with this were-creature concept?"

Boone whined in the back.

I turned around and found his standing up with a big, goofy doggie grin on his face. To Alex, I said, "There is nothing weird about thinking werewolves might be real. Everything else creepy and nightmarish seems to be real. Case in point, me."

Alex made a strangled noise. "I'll take your kind of nightmare any day."

What was it about me that everyone found so not terrifying? I had fangs and magic and a living sword that was insanely sharp—most of the time.

"How many people do I have to kill dead with my awesome magic sword before I'm considered scary?"

"You're up to one injured and one dead so far?"

I nodded.

"I don't know, a few hundred?" Alex grinned. "You don't exactly strike dread in the hearts of men."

I sniffed as he pulled to the curb in front of a tidy little cottage-style home. "But I could. I just need to work on my rep."

"Yeah, sure." Alex looked over his shoulder at Boone. "Is it just me, or is someone ready to work?"

But Boone was more than ready to work. He had his massive muzzle smashed against the tiny crack in the back-seat window, and I could hear the huffing sound of him inhaling.

The longer we were parked, the louder Boone's huffing breaths were getting, and he'd started a low, persistent whine that escaped with each exhalation. And that was when I realized that maybe Boone hadn't been getting enough exercise—or fun—at my house.

"Oops." I gave Alex a guilty look. "It's possible he's not used to being cooped up for days at a time."

"I'm sure he's not. Have you not been doing anything with him?"

Boone swung his big head around so fast that his ears smacked the back of the passenger seat and he woofed excit-edly. Then he was back at the wind, inhaling through the crack again.

"We've hung out on the sofa together," I said in a small voice.

"Good grief, Mallory. I'll come by and take him for a run a few times a week."

"Deal." After Alex was out of the car, I said to Boone, "I love you, buddy, but I'm not running unless chased. Actu-ally, I have a wicked sharp sword that comes when called, so —basically—I'm not running."

Boone turned to give me a mournful look.

"What? Alex is totally gonna hook you up." I hopped out of the car before those deep brown eyes and droopy folds of skin had me promising to become a marathoner.

I got Boone harnessed in just a few seconds. I'd practiced putting it on him at the house, because I didn't want to look like an idiot fumbling around with the straps. I was glad for the practice, because I was nervous.

"All right, Boone-dog, we can do this." I had no clue why I was nervous. It was the poor dog doing most of the work.

Alex motioned to the Escalade that I'd failed to notice parked across the street. "Anton is inside waiting for us."

Boone made a hacking nose.

"I knew there was a reason we get along so well." I rubbed Boone's head, trying to dispel my jitters.

We both shared a dislike for the burly Mr. Clean lookalike. I wasn't sure what Boone's reasons were, but mine were the obvious sort. He was never nice to me and had made my transformation into a vamp much more difficult. He'd refrained from killing me, so he had that going for him...but not much else.

I grasped the end of Boone's leash firmly. "Okay, go sniff, Boone-dog."

Not like he wasn't already—his muzzle had been lifted and his nostrils were working overtime while I'd harnessed him and the whole while we'd been standing next to the car —but on my cue, he took off at a trot, his back end swaying in what looked like a waddle and his nose hovering a few inches from the ground.

We cruised through the grassy yard, up into the flower beds next to the house, and then followed the house around to the right until we hit a fence. I thought poor Boone was going to smack his head into it, but at the last second he stopped and lifted his nose, following the line of the fence upward.

He gave a full-body shake and turned back the way we'd come, not pausing to investigate the shrubbery we'd already passed. When we hit the paved path leading up to the front door, he paused then continued forward and did a brief investigation of the left side of the house. Very quickly, he returned to the paved path and paused there, flicking a glance over his shoulder at me.

It was only then that I noticed Alex chatting with a small group of people. I hadn't realized the neighborhood was so busy with foot traffic: joggers, moms with strollers, walkers, dog walkers...

Oh my.

I whispered to Boone, "I hope you got what you needed, because we've just become neighborhood gossip."

Boone headed to the front door, so I was taking that as a yes. When we reached the door, it opened wide, and a tall, broad, muscular guy with a clean-shaven head stood there waiting for us to come in.

"Anton," I said curtly.

"Mallory," he replied with an equal lack of warmth.

Boone took one sniff of Anton and sneezed on him.

"That dog is disgusting."

I pressed my lips together, trying not to grin. That was one way to ease my nerves. "Did you ever consider that he might find *you* disgusting?"

Boone's tail thumped against the doorframe with a great deal of vigor. I'd say that was agreement. Boone tugged on the leash and pulled me inside past Anton. Once we'd cleared the door and given Anton plenty of space, I detached Boone's leash from his harness. He didn't linger; instead he lowered his head and started his interior search.

I gave Anton a parting glance as he headed back outside to join Alex. And to think that Rachael—beautiful, intelligent, rich Rachael—had a thing for Anton. Apparently intelligence wasn't an accurate predictor of good taste in men.

Alex came inside as Boone searched the living room, which was good news for me—because I wasn't feeling so good and was glad for a little moral support. As soon as I'd entered the living room, my nerves had worsened. A sense of dread settled in the pit of my stomach. I clenched Boone's wadded-up leather leash between my fingers.

The once tidy room had a superficially chaotic look: the decorative couch pillows on the floor, the coffee table off-center, a fluffy throw on the floor, and an armchair tipped on its side.

My stomach churned. This was a little girl's home. A single mother and her child lived here.

"I really don't feel well," I whispered. I hadn't meant to say that, hated feeling weak around people who were all sturdier, stronger, and more magical than me. But I felt that bad.

I couldn't take my eyes off the room. I should be watching Boone, but something about the pretty silk pillows, with their bright, cheerful colors, strewn across the floor...I just couldn't look away.

"Do you need to sit down? You don't—"

"It's fine." I shook my head. I'd seen so much worse than this—so why did this scene bother me so much? "There's not even any blood."

"No. No blood. We're hopeful Akira is alive, and will continue to base our search on that assumption until we find...until we have definitive proof that she isn't."

I shivered. They needed a body. For it to be murder, there needed to be a body—even in the Society's archaic justice system.

Boone cruised past me, looking relaxed and comfort-able, and headed to the kitchen. I shook off the odd, uncomfortable sense of foreboding that had overcome me and followed him.

"And if there's never a body?" I asked, watching as Boone ran his nose along all the crevices and corners of the kitchen.

"Then a witch-verified confession will do, but that assumes we can find the killer without the evidence a body would give us."

Boone flipped a U and headed to the opposite side of the house where the bedrooms were located, and Alex and I followed.

Watching Boone move swiftly down the hallway, I hoped it wasn't a killer he was hunting. Kidnapping was bad...but murder...

I squeezed the leash in my hands. "I really don't want to think about finding anything but Akira alive and well."

Alex pressed his lips together and silently followed Boone into the master bedroom.

His silence broke my heart for that poor little twelve-year-old girl.

7

PSYCHIC TEXT MESSAGING

Boone gave the bedrooms and bathroom a cursory search, and showed no lingering interest in any of the rooms. When he passed through the bedroom Akira was using as an office, I pointed to the laptop on the desk, and Alex collected it.

Boone finished his search of the small house with a second trip around the living room, the only room where I'd felt a deep sense of discomfort.

I hesitated in the hallway leading to the living room. "Is it possible for an event to leave a physical impression on a room?"

Alex, several feet ahead of me, stopped and pivoted around to face me. "Why do you ask?"

But he looked like he knew, so I crossed my arms and waited.

"Yeah, maybe."

"Don't tell me," I said, "it's like the precognition enhancement that you swear doesn't exist. Rumors abound, but there's no proof."

"Basically. Well, a little more proof than for precognition." His gaze circled around the room. "You feel that here, in this room? For a psychic stain to result, I'd expect a horrific triggering event. But it doesn't look like that much happened here."

Which was true. While there was certainly evidence of a struggle, only a few items had been displaced. It didn't look like the scene of a murder or torture. My brain blanked on other things that Alex might label as horrific.

Regardless of what had or hadn't happened there, the room *felt* wrong. It felt invaded. Violated.

"You never explained what a kitsune is." I couldn't figure out another explanation. Akira must have left that impression upon the room, because the impressions were a victim's —not a kidnapper's.

"A fox spirit. A kitsune inhabits both the spirit realm and the physical one, but is always a woman in her physical form." Alex tipped his head. "I think that means kitsune are always women, but I'm not really sure how that works. You think Akira left some psychic mark?"

"What else you got?" I eyed the invisible barrier between the hallway and the living room—one I wasn't convinced existed solely in my mind—with some misgiving. "Do you think a kitsune could do that?"

"I don't know. I'm not sure what she can do. I know she has a spirit form because of my own magical predilections —not because she's shared that with me. We're not close."

"Could you leave a psychic mark on a room?"

He ran his hand through his hair. He took a few seconds to answer, but then said, "I hope not."

"I get that your magic is private—very private—but I need a little more. Something's going on here, in this room, and it might be a clue. Give me something."

"Look, I know her true reflection is a fox—that's how I

knew she was a kitsune when I met her. Your true reflection is just"—he shook his head—"it's just you: bright, beautiful. You. Wembley's is fierce, sad. And Akira's is a wily red fox."

I stood, hovering on the edge of the room, and my heart gave a little tug. He thought I was beautiful—or my true reflection was. I was wowed, even though I didn't really understand what a true reflection was. Maybe an aura? But now was not the time for me to melt because of a few nice words.

Wily. Akira was wily.

"It's a message," I said. "It has to be. Do your spirit-reading thing."

"If you mean you want me to check the area for spirits, I would have sensed any if they were here."

"Check," I insisted.

He looked toward the front door where Anton had been stationed earlier.

"You're safe to do your thing; he's still outside." I was surprised Alex hadn't already reached out to the resident spirit entities. That was one of his enhancements. Actually, I was kinda fuzzy on exactly what Alex could do besides kick some rear with a sword, whisper open the most difficult locks, and talk to spirit entities. He was freakishly private.

"Whoa." Alex took a step backward.

I blinked. "You did something. What did you do? The nasty sense of dread just vanished." So much so that I joined him in the middle of the living room.

"I think Akira left me a message, and you intercepted it."

Which made me squirm. First, how did *I* pick up on it when Alex didn't? And second, how did Akira know about Alex's super-secret connection to the land of spirits, demons, and elementals? Although that did seem to be less of a secret than Alex would like.

"Please tell me that the message was more than your skin crawling." Or a sense of impending doom. Or a feeling of dread. Yeah, I'd definitely felt all of those, but it seemed redundant to trot out the whole list.

"There was a sense of her fear, certainly. But there was a message, a series of images, actually. The first was a faceless man. The second a phone, and the third was Michelle."

Parsing that combination into a message made my brain hurt. "I have no idea what that means. She must have left the message specifically for you—who else is going to stumble into the house and pick up on spirit vibes?" I nimbly ignored the fact that *I* had...sort of. "If the pictures are for you, maybe they contain a message only you can decipher."

Alex looked frustrated. "I don't even know how she knew I'd be able to pick up the message. I've never been on the receiving end of a psychic text."

I couldn't help it. I had to stop and admire Akira's cleverness. "Text via the spirit world. You have to admit, it's brilliant."

Some of the stress eased from his face. "Since I got it, I'll agree: brilliant. Although risky, since she couldn't be guaranteed I'd be assigned the case."

I put my hands on my hips. "Really?"

"What?" He actually looked clueless.

"You're involved in every serious case, Alex. The emergency response unit seems like a bunch of slackers, because every time I turn around, there you are."

"And how is it that every time you turn around, there's a crisis?"

My hands fell from my hips. It was hard to take a righteously judgmental stance when faced with my own flaws.

"So I'm a little nosy." I shrugged with one shoulder and gave him my most winning smile.

"Stones, glass houses..." He lifted his hands. "That's all I'm saying."

I wrinkled my nose at him and then said, "Truce. But that brings us right back around to the same question: what the heck do those pictures mean?"

Boone moaned and stood up. He'd been stretched out on his side—possibly even napping—for the last several minutes. Boone must not have picked up on the funky vibe any more than Alex. The psychic goo of nasty feelings just wanted to stick to me. What luck.

I rubbed Boone's silky ears. "Do you know who did this?" I indicated the mess in the living room.

Boone dropped down on his haunches and gave me a droopy, sad expression.

"Boone." Boone's head swiveled to Alex. "Did you pick up on the scent of the person who did this?"

Boone's tail thudded against the floor. Not the most enthusiastic response I'd seen, but a start.

"So, you could recognize the scent again?" More tail wagging greeted my question. "But you can't attach the scent to someone you already know?"

Boone stared mournfully back.

"That's good news, buddy, because we're about to hit our second stop, and we'll need you to check for that scent." Boone perked up, and his tail thwacked the floor. The poor guy had been lounging on my newly pet-proofed sofa way too much the last few days. I looked at Alex. "We're done."

"Yeah. Headquarters from here, because I need to give Cornelius Akira's message and sketch the faceless guy—what I can remember of him."

At some point, I'd clipped Boone's leash into a loop and

slung it across my body. I unhooked it and attached it to his collar again. It got weirder and weirder for me to have him on a leash, like I was dehumanizing him. Which I was, because he was a dog. Sort of.

Boone hopped up and with a jaunty, waddling trot, headed to the door. He didn't seem to be developing the complex that I was over his leash.

Alex opened the door for me. After Boone and I slipped past him, he said, "I should mention, Cornelius hired both of us."

I stopped on the front porch of the house. "You negotiated a deal for me?"

He turned to close the front door, avoiding my gaze. "Yeah. I didn't think you'd mind."

Mind? I felt positively warm and fuzzy. First I was beautiful, now I was getting paid to do something I'd have done for free: help reunite a little girl with her mother. And—bonus!—I got to satisfy my blazing curiosity and give my bored hound a job. It was win, win, and win some more, so far as I was concerned.

I replied as neutrally as I could, "Sure. That's fine."

And I tried not to do a little happy dance.

8

THE APP OF (BRADLEY'S) DOOM

Cornelius wasn't flashing his liquid mercury eyes at me. They were their normal blue-grey. That was a start, because even a hint of silver meant he was trying to scare me into behaving.

A missing mother, a temporarily (I hoped) motherless child, and a potentially missing Elvis impersonator... With all that, did I even care if Cornelius flashed his scary silver eyes at me?

At least the pressure wasn't getting to Boone. He lounged on Cornelius's imported oriental rug with reckless abandon. No drool that I could see, so that was good.

Movement in my peripheral vision caught my attention, and I saw that Alex had slumped in his chair and stretched out his long legs in front of him.

I was the odd man out here, since everyone seemed to feel comfortable in Cornelius's office except me. I sat a little taller in my chair. A visit to Cornelius always reminded me of being called into the vice principal's office for a stern talking to. My stomach flip-flopped when I thought about where Akira might be right now. A lecture from a cranky old assassin—creepy glowing eyes or not—was a darn sight better than being kidnapped and taken away from my child. That comparison lent some perspective to the situation.

"Ms. Andrews?" Cornelius did not sound pleased.

"Yes, I'm sorry—what was the question?"

"If you have any thoughts concerning the message Akira Mori left."

"What about it?" I asked in a small voice.

"I believe the most relevant question is: what does it mean?"

Since I'd twisted my brain in knots on the drive here trying to answer that question and come up with bupkis, I wasn't dying to respond. As if I didn't feel guilty enough already.

Alex leaned forward and pulled his chair up to the edge of Cornelius's desk. "Pass me a piece of paper."

Once he had a sheet of printer paper and a pen, he started to sketch, his pen flying across the page. "The phone was a cell, a smartphone. I couldn't make out the screen because of a bright glare bouncing off it."

I perked up. "That's weird. You didn't mention that before: that the face of the phone was showing."

Alex continued to sketch and said, "I couldn't see anything, so there wasn't anything to— Ah. Foolish of me." He put the pen down and flipped his sketch around for Cornelius to see.

"Yes," Cornelius agreed. At his nod, Alex picked it up and passed it to me.

On the page was a figure, clearly a man, but with no facial features visible. Alex had drawn a haze around the man's face. His clothing was casual: a worn T-shirt, jeans, and sturdy hiking-type shoes. In fact, with the exception of the face, there was quite a lot of detail, including the words "Def Leppard" emblazoned across the shirt.

"Okay, that's weird. First, who can sketch this well?" I glanced at Alex; he didn't *quite* roll his eyes. "And second, two different images with the most distinguishing characteristics erased. That is not an accident. I don't suppose the phone was pink with a bedazzled case or anything like that?"

"No. Some kind of black smartphone. But you're right that the distinguishing features being erased is too much of a coincidence. I'd say Akira was trying to give us the identity of her attacker with those first two images."

"And he was blocking them, which indicates he was prepared with knowledge of her abilities and had some means to counteract her psychic message—in part." Cornelius steepled his fingers together. "Concerning, since kitsune are hardly common, and their abilities not widely known."

A picture of a smartphone... An uncomfortable feeling crept up my spine. "What can kitsune do?"

"They have the ability of persuasion and illusion, traditionally trickster characteristics. But unlike coyotes, you don't see them using their abilities to entertain or steal."

Alex arched a brow. "Not to paint an entire group with too broad a brush."

Cornelius frowned at him. "Coyotes are much more common than kitsune, and we're speaking in generalities here. You can't deny that coyotes have more...hustle than kitsune. Either a cultural difference or something tied to their inherent abilities, but there is a difference."

"Okay, but either way, what about the message?" I asked. I felt like I was stepping into the middle of a fight between Mom and Dad. Awkward.

"They're shape shifters, of a sort—"

"I knew it!" But I pressed my lips together and tried to look contrite when I saw Cornelius shoot me a disapproving look.

"As I was saying, shape shifters of a sort. Kitsune have a fox spirit, but only limited ability to interact on this plane in their animal form. But they can communicate with the spirit world."

I raised my hand, Bradley-style. When Cornelius gave a sharp nod, I said, "Could that be why the message was in pictures? Foxes don't speak, right?" I wrinkled my nose. "Although maybe magical foxes do."

"No, that's a valid consideration," Cornelius said. "Akira would be limited to her fox form in the spirit world. But even if the pictures were left because they were her only means of communicating, that still leaves the question of their interpretation."

And we were back to a blank face, a twelve-tear old girl, and a cell phone. A cell phone...which was usually chock-full of apps.

Uh-oh. Bradley's app. We needed to be talking about anything but that cell phone. This time, Alex did kick me in the shins. Gently. Sort of. I wiped the panic from my face.

"You think her attacker had inside knowledge of her skills that allowed him to prepare for the eventuality of a psychic message?" Alex asked.

"Perhaps." Cornelius leaned back in his chair and clasped his hands over his stomach. "The alternative is certainly concerning."

I practically bounced in my chair. "What alternative?"

"The alternative, Ms. Andrews, is that the attacker has a psychic presence so powerful that he was able to alter perception without focused intent."

While that sounded bad, it was Cornelius's grim tone that sold me on the badness. The words were just blah, blah, blah.

Alex sighed. "You've got a motion-sensing security light at the house." I nodded, and he continued, "When someone sets it off, the light comes on. The only other alternative is to leave the light all the time."

I nodded, but I still didn't get it.

"Okay, how about this. You know how I look for spirits, demons, elementals? That consumes magical energy. But if I could see them without trying, if they simply appeared, that would require more power because I would be looking all the time."

"Got it." Pretty much. "That's not common? That someone can run their magical battery all the time?"

"No, that's not a common," Cornelius replied, looking curiously between the two of us. "So you're familiar with Alex's particular talents?"

I knew I had a deer-in-headlights look. I could feel the burn of my eyeballs, but I couldn't make myself blink. That magically spiked promise that Alex and I had made to keep each other's secrets hadn't covered my response in situations like these. I pressed my lips together tighter, because I didn't want to get zapped for an accidental infraction.

"She knows," Alex said, and I exhaled a sigh of relief. "Since it's highly unlikely our subject has off-the-charts psychic energy, I'm betting he was prepared. Does Akira have any enemies within the Society? I'm not aware of any unsettled disputes, but—"

"No." Cornelius waved a hand dismissively. "She wasn't the sort."

"Isn't," I corrected. "She isn't the sort. For the sake of my mental health, we're going with her being alive unless we find evidence to the contrary."

"But back to the point"—Alex shot me a loaded look —"someone with intimate knowledge of Akira's skills did this, and that list can't be long."

I tried to keep my expression blank. Fingers crossed I was wrong, but I couldn't help thinking of Bradley's app. Created as a companion to a board game, it was basically a wiki of Austin's finest paranormal freaks, including my mostly peace-loving roomie Wembley, a.k.a. Einarr the former Viking berserker. Bradley hadn't known he was treading on dangerous ground, because he'd been ignorant of the Society's existence at the time. He'd relied upon a mysterious journal provided by his anonymous client for the app's content, and hadn't for a second thought the people referenced truly existed—until he met Einarr.

With any luck, Cornelius wouldn't make the connection, because I liked Bradley's brain just as it was: weird but unscrambled by the Society's magical memory-excision techniques. He'd agreed not to spill what he'd learned, and Cornelius had, in turn, agreed not fry any of Bradley's brain cells.

"Ms. Andrews, do you have any other thoughts to share, or would you prefer to continue daydreaming?"

Better that Cornelius think I was being scatterbrained than realize I'd been stressing about Bradley's brains being magically sautéed. "Nope. Well, I guess—did you get anything pertinent from Michelle?"

Alex coughed. That was an improvement over kicking my shins, his usual method of silencing me. Obviously, I'd missed that part of the conversation earlier when I'd taken a little stress break from reality and mentally revisited my wayward high school years.

Cornelius started to answer, stopped himself, then looked at Alex. "You asked for her; you deal with her."

Alex nodded, not seeming terribly put out by my spacey behavior. "I'll update her on the way to Patrick's. If we're done?"

Cornelius inclined his head, and I hopped up out of my chair like someone had poked me. I took a breath and slowed down, because I didn't have any reason to be rushing out Cornelius's office...so far as he knew.

Boone got up, stretched, and then followed Alex and me out into the hall. Once the door was closed, I bounced up and down on my toes.

Alex put a hand on my shoulder, like I'd float away if he didn't hold me in place. "I know. Coffee in my office before we leave?"

That was code for keep my mouth shut until we were further from Cornelius's office. And I did—for a good thirty or forty seconds.

I inhaled to speak, and Alex cut me off. "We came in because I wanted to interview Michelle myself, and I figured we could do it together after we updated Cornelius. And I was hoping he'd have some insight into the message she left."

"Which is all nifty—except for Akira's message possibly implicating Bradley's app, and Cornelius now being on notice of that fact. How do we keep Bradley's brain in its currently odd but lovable condition if Cornelius goes on a witch hunt?" I increased my pace, practically speed-walking down the hall. Boone had to trot to keep up.

"We're in a hurry—but not quite that much. We still have to speak with Michelle before we can save Bradley."

And if that language wasn't telling... "I knew it. You think Cornelius might give Bradley grief."

"I don't know what he'll do, and that's enough reason to keep an eye on your buddy. We need to go pick him up before we head to Patrick's place."

I stopped. "I'm not sure how an outing is gonna go over with Bradley.

Alex didn't stop. Over his shoulder, he said two little words: "Memory excision."

"Nuts. Where is Michelle?"

"She's in the office with Francis waiting for us, which you'd have heard earlier if you hadn't been daydreaming."

"Hallelujah. I can get a cup of coffee." I could already feel the yummy buzz just thinking about it.

"Because coffee makes everything better?"

"You got it. And I wasn't daydreaming; I was a little distracted."

"Right. I won't ask by what." Alex opened his office door and waited for me to precede him.

The first thing I saw as I walked in was a teary-eyed girl in a school uniform sitting on his futon.

Coffee wasn't going to make this any better. Not even a little bit.

9

KIDS SAY THE DARNEDEST THINGS

Michelle was beautiful. Even with damp eyes and a red nose, she was stop-you-in-your-tracks gorgeous. Her straight, glossy, dark brown hair was cut in a long, asymmetrical bob that swung forward as she dabbed her eyes with a handkerchief.

She stood up as we approached, and I realized she was taller than me. At twelve, that's rough for a girl. Good grief. Where was my brain? Rough was having your mom disappear with no idea if she was still alive or not. I could feel my eyes to start to burn with sympathetic tears.

Alex touched the small of my back—just for a second, but it was enough for me to remember why we were here. I took a breath and continued forward.

"You're Mallory and Alex? Francis said you'd want to talk to me about my mom."

Francis emerged from the kitchen nook with a steaming mug. Catching Alex's eye, he said, "I thought some hot chocolate was called for."

Alex nodded. Pulling the two chairs clustered near his desk closer, he said, "Please have a seat, Michelle."

Francis delivered Michelle's hot chocolate and then took a seat at the opposite end of the futon. Alex and I sat in the chairs. I scanned the room and found that Boone had planted himself directly in front of the door. Anyone coming or going would do it over a sprawling red hound.

I turned back around to find Michelle huddled over her hot chocolate, both hands wrapped around it.

"Francis and Cornelius already asked if Mom has any enemies, or if I've noticed her acting oddly lately. But I really don't know anyone who would want to hurt her." Her brow furrowed. "Or how they could."

"What do you mean?" I asked.

Michelle set her hot chocolate down on the coffee table and clasped her hands around her balled-up hankie. "She's powerful, nine-tailed. For a kitsune, that's a high level of physical and psychic achievement." Michelle sniffed and wiped her eyes. "Oh, and she's an MMA fighter."

I blinked. Even with red blotches, I could see that Michelle had flawless skin, big doe eyes…she didn't look like the daughter of a mixed martial arts fighter. And as soon as I thought it, I realized how idiotic that thought was. "The last few days she's been her normal self?"

Michelle's face crumpled. She leaned forward and covered her face with her handkerchief.

I looked at Alex for some clue as to what I'd said. The girl was shattered.

We waited for her to recover. Eventually she said with a small, desperate laugh, "My mom is perfect. Strong, kind, smart, the kind of woman I can only hope to be someday." She took a breath. "If something was wrong, she would *never* have said. Or shown any signs, not unless she thought I should know." She wiped her eyes again. "I don't remember the last time I told her I loved her. I wasn't even nice to her when she dropped me at school this morning."

I didn't know the woman, but it was clear from everyone's opinion that she'd been a wonderful mother. She must love her daughter very much. "You know she—"

Michelle's anguished gaze met mine, silencing me. "I know."

Alex asked, "What about appointments today?"

Michelle took a breath and then said, "Any of her appointments would be on her calendar. On her computer. Did you find it?"

"We did," I reassured her. "One of the emergency response men is delivering it to our expert. I don't suppose you know the password?" When she shook her head, I asked, "Is your mom an Elvis fan?"

Michelle perked up. "Yeah, hardcore. How did you know that?"

Alex leaned forward. "Did she know a local impersonator, a guy who does shows in town?"

"Do you mean Patrick? At least, that's his name now." Michelle's glance darted between the two of us, and finally landed on Francis. "Patrick wouldn't hurt my mom. He's a really nice guy." When Francis didn't respond, she turned back to Alex with a look of disbelief. "They play tennis together."

"We're not accusing him of anything," Alex said. "We just need to know what their connection is. What can you tell us about him?"

Michelle's face scrunched up as she thought about it "I'm sure nothing the Society doesn't already know." When Alex gave her an encouraging nod, she said, "He just got back in town recently. I only know because Mom dug her tennis racket out of the closet. He's the only one she plays with."

"Because she's an MMA fighter?" The question slipped out, and I almost apologized.

But Michelle grinned. "Crazy, right? She refuses to comment on the philosophies or the industry, just says it's good fun." Her grin widened, and the room practically shone with the light of her smile. "And she kicks a lot of butt."

We needed to find this girl's mother.

Alex pulled a card out of his wallet and handed it to Michelle. "I understand that Francis is going to stay with you for a little while."

Her expression turned neutral. "Yeah, no one's been able to get in touch with my dad."

I did a double take. Why had I thought her dad was dead? Really strange when I thought back on the little I knew of him. Alex hadn't said so, only that he was no longer in Akira and Michelle's lives. "Where does your dad live?"

She shrugged. "We haven't talked in years. Mom says she doesn't think it's a good idea, like she's discouraged him from having a relationship with me. And I believed her...for a while. I finally figured out he didn't care, and she didn't want me to know that."

Alex stood up, and I followed suit.

"If you think of anything..." Alex glanced at the business card in her hand.

Michelle nodded. We were about halfway to the door when she called out, "Oh, just a second. If you have questions about Patrick, you should ask Ralph. He knows about as much as anyone about Patrick's new identity. He's not a Society member, so he doesn't know who, or what, Patrick is. But he's way more of a fan than Mom."

Alex and I shared a look. He asked, "How do you know Ralph?"

"Ralph? Everyone who's into Elvis impersonators knows Ralph. He's a part of the scene." Michelle's face pinched into a confused expression. "You think Ralph... No way. No *way*. He's a wimp; Mom would kick his butt. And he's mundane. Like, one hundred percent, you know?"

"That's cool. Thanks for the heads-up." I grabbed Alex's arm and pulled. He didn't move, didn't even notice until I sank my nails into his bicep.

"Thanks," Alex said. "Call if you think of anything else."

Michelle nodded and we made our escape.

As soon as Boone's tail cleared the door and Alex shut it, I asked, "Super-hearing?"

"No. She's basically human at this point. What's with the claws?"

"I thought it was better that we didn't bring every person of her acquaintance under a cloud of suspicion, and the claws were because you weren't listening." I walked through the door of Bits, Baubles, and Toadstools that Alex held open for me. "She might look like a young woman, but she's a child."

"She was quick to defend both Patrick and Ralph."

"*I* don't want to believe that people I know would do terrible things, so I'm guessing that would be even more difficult for a twelve-year-old—regardless of how mature she may look and act." I waved at Mandy as we passed through the store.

Alex gave her a quick nod and picked up his pace. "Come on. We need to pick up Bradley pronto."

Bradley. I'd been so distracted that he'd slipped down in the priority queue for a brief moment. But if Cornelius thought Bradley was a liability, he'd have Bradley's grey matter magicked in a heartbeat. Something that would be lot more difficult if Alex and I were with him. I picked up my pace and tried to think of a convincing argument to get my not-quite-agoraphobic sidekick out of his condo.

10

SAVING BRADLEY'S BRAIN

B radley opened the door with a suspicion-filled look.

I never showed up unannounced, because I was halfway civilized—even if I did have fangs. And texting from the parking garage about two minutes before appearing at his door didn't exactly qualify as announcing myself.

Add to that the big red beast I'd brought with me, and Bradley had to have some idea trouble was afoot.

I smiled. "Any chance you've made progress with Akira's laptop?"

"Yes." Very slowly, he opened the door wider and let us in, but he didn't take his eyes off Boone.

We stopped just inside the door, and Boone settled down at my feet. I didn't think Bradley would deal well with a shedding dog—and not at all with a drooling hound—cruising through his condo.

After Bradley shut the door. Alex asked, "What did you find?"

"Not much security. I cracked the password with a few Google searches." Bradley looked uncomfortable, but there were no disapproving looks for the missing Akira. That was downright sensitive of him. "She didn't have any appointments. Her workday was broken up into several blocks of time, each assigned to a project. And her business dealt with low-risk clients. No big-name clients, no risky investments. Her average client is middle class, risk-averse, and financially conservative."

Not like we expected to hear otherwise, but finding a suspect or two besides Patrick-Elvis and Heckler Ralph would have been nice. Speaking of... "Any chance you can get into her contacts?"

Bradley nodded, watching Boone as he rolled onto his side. "Easy."

"We need to know about Ralph and Patrick-Elvis," I said.

"Patrick Twombly," Alex said as Bradley headed into his office. "And also Wes Sheffield."

Bradley came back with the laptop. "Will he stay?" he asked, eyeballing Boone.

"Stay?" I asked Boone.

Boone thumped his tail.

I gave Bradley a reassuring smile. "Absolutely. And he's housetrained, promise."

Bradley set up the laptop on the kitchen table. "Akira Mori uses a simple email program to store her contacts." He sat down and started to type. After a few seconds, he looked up with a frown on his face. "She has both Patrick Twombly and Ralph Dukat in her contacts. You think her disappearance is connected to Patrick's?"

I nodded enthusiastically—maybe bounced a little. "I do."

Alex refrained from rolling his eyes—barely. "I'd like to confirm Patrick's disappearance before we start making connections. And if he is missing, we have no way of knowing if he's a victim or a suspect without more information. What about Sheffield?"

"Oh, yes," I said. "That's Michelle's dad. The Society has been trying to reach him all afternoon." Then I remembered what she'd said about her dad not caring to keep in touch with her. "Or maybe staying with Francis would be better. Francis is lovely."

Alex stared at me.

"What?"

"You don't even know Francis."

Bradley interrupted our little disagreement with a raised hand.

Since I seemed to have picked up the habit myself, I could hardly tell him he needn't bother. "What's up?"

"There's no contact information for Wes Sheffield on Akira Mori's laptop. Do you want me to run a background on him? Dig up a current address and phone number?"

"Can you do it on the road?" Alex asked.

Bradley's fingers stilled on the laptop. "Why?"

"You need to come with us, just for a little while." Possibly an exaggeration, maybe even a fib—but I *hoped* it wouldn't be long.

"Why would I want to do that?" Bradley looked at me like I'd lost my mind.

"It's possible the app you developed is creating some difficulties, so we need to keep an eye on you—just for a little while—to make sure that Cornelius and his henchmen don't sneak you off for a secret lobotomy." As I spoke, Bradley pushed his chair out and stood up.

"Better an outing with us than magical memory excision," Alex said.

"No." Bradley crossed his arms.

I paused and considered his response. Were we that

bad? He'd been out with us a few nights ago, and I thought we'd managed not to traumatize him too badly.

"Wouldn't you prefer to keep all of your"—I indicated my head vaguely with my hands—"stuff that makes you *you*? There's no telling what Cornelius's people will do to you once they get inside your head and start tinkering."

What I didn't say was that Bradley was already a little scrambled—in an adorable, unique-to-him way—but also in a way that meant he struggled with the realities of social interaction. Of anyone I knew, he really didn't need to have someone making magical adjustments to his grey cells.

Alex nodded. "It's theoretically a targeted memory alteration, but things happen. Especially with mundanes."

"I didn't do anything wrong; they can't do that." His chin, already firm, now jutted out.

On the one hand it was refreshing to encounter someone who had such abiding faith in the rule of law, justice, fairness—whatever it was that made Bradley believe that Cornelius would actually do the right thing.

On the other hand, I knew Cornelius and the Society.

"Forget about the app and the Society," Alex said. "Don't you want to help us search Elvis's house for clues?"

I could hear Boone's tail thump in excitement from across the room. Too bad Bradley wasn't looking as excited. Probably because we'd already pissed him off with the whole "let us protect you from an unjust lobotomy" argument. Neither of us had realized how oversized Bradley's sense of fair play was.

In retrospect, I realized Elvis and sleuthing should have been our first suggestion. In my mind, avoiding almost certain bodily injury trumped the awesomeness of sleuthing. Barely, but it was only close because—speaking of brain scrambling—I'd become obscenely nosy after my vamp transformation had tinkered with the inner workings of my brain.

While Bradley looked interested in the prospect of investigating Patrick-Elvis's possible disappearance, his arms were still crossed.

Nuts.

Time to lay it all out there, to get friendly with my feelings. If only I could cry on cue...

I looked him directly in the eye and said, "Bradley, I'm worried sick something will happen to you, and it will be all my fault. I couldn't live with the guilt if Cornelius's henchmen hurt you. And I do think it could happen."

"They can't do that." And he seemed quite convinced of the truth of his statement.

"But let's just imagine that the Society can do something terrible, something unjust, even though they're basically the paranormal government."

"Not basically," Alex said. "The Society *is* the local government for the enhanced community."

I shot him an annoyed, "not helping" look, and he looked up at the ceiling. Rolling his eyes? Praying for guidance? I wasn't sure.

I shifted away from Alex, deliberately excluding him from my conversation with Bradley. "Let's imagine the Society might hurt you, even though you haven't done anything wrong. If they did, it would be my fault because I got you involved with the Society."

Bradley frowned, glanced at Boone still lying near the front door, and frowned even more.

"Please, please come with us. For my sanity. To save me untold hours of guilt-ridden regret." Okay, maybe a little thick—but I *would* feel terrible if something happened to him.

Finally, he said, "I get to ride shotgun. Does your car smell like dog?"

And I let out a sigh of relief. I grinned at him and fibbed. "It's not too bad."

"Am I allowed to speak now?" Alex asked.

Turning to once again include him in the conversation, I smiled brightly and said, "Sure."

"Do you have a file on Patrick Twombly?" Alex asked Bradley.

"Yes. I printed it out for you, just in case you asked."

Not a stalker my rear end. But I pressed my lips together and kept my thoughts to myself. That was, after all, Bradley's function in our unofficial little sleuthing crew. He was the techie, hacker, stalker guy. Or, as he preferred to be called, my sidekick.

He met us at the front door with a file folder and a thumb drive. He handed the thumb drive to me and the file to Alex.

Alex and I switched.

"That's odd," Bradley said.

I looked at Bradley for some clue as to his meaning, but he just looked confused.

I shrugged.

Bradley pointed at Alex and said, "He's over seven hundred years old, but you're the one who wants the paper copy."

My mouth opened. Then closed. I took a breath, meaning to say something—but what? I exhaled without speaking...and I didn't look at Alex.

Because this was Bradley, and Bradley got his facts right.

"Thanks, Bradley," Alex said.

"No problem." Bradley wasn't the kind of guy who easily picked up on sarcasm.

Boone got up and nudged my fingers with his nose. I pressed his big head against my leg and scratched under his collar.

"All righty, then, let's go," I said, giving Boone a final scratch—and still avoiding Alex.

"Mallory—"

I shook my head and motioned to the door. I needed a little time to process that one of my closest friends—because Alex had become a friend—hadn't just been hanging around for a few decades. He was an old, *ancient* dude. I groaned and shook my head when I realized Wembley considered Alex "young." I couldn't even begin to fathom how old Wembley must be.

Alex opened the door and walked out into the hall without another word.

Weirdly, it was Bradley who carried the conversation while we took the elevator down to the parking garage. Now that he was committed to the Patrick-Elvis outing—and leaving the condo in general—he didn't mind sharing how excited he was about seeing the inside of Patrick-Elvis's house.

"Of course, I know the neighborhood. It's quiet, secluded, and a little expensive without being ostentatious." Bradley sounded like he was reading from a sales brochure. "And the exterior of the house is very well maintained. Not that I'd expect anything else."

How Bradley—"of course"—knew Patrick Elvis's neighborhood, when he rarely left his condo, I didn't want to know. We'd need to have a chat about the extent of his admiration and how he expressed it. There was fandom and there was crazy dude. Bradley tended to struggle with such distinctions.

And then we were approaching my car, and I wasn't tied

up in knots anymore. A little wiggy, but I could at least make eye contact with Alex now.

"Hey, coming at you," I said a second before I chucked my keys at Alex.

He caught them—because the man had mad hand-eye coordination. "Thanks." Except I was pretty sure he wasn't talking about letting him drive.

A few minutes later I realized, first, that I'd never ridden in a car with Bradley before and, second, that I hoped to never again.

The normally reticent Bradley kept up a steady stream of chatter, commenting on almost everything. Not in itself a problem, but many of his comments held a certain backseat-driving flavor. Especially annoying, since Alex was a preter-naturally good driver.

Finally, I interrupted him. "Hey, Bradley, why don't you give us a summary of Patrick-Elvis's file?"

"Why do you call him Patrick-Elvis?" Bradley looked over his shoulder at me. "Either name within the context of the conversation would be sufficient."

"Does it matter? That's just how I think of him." Bradley was not satisfied by that response, so I quickly explained before he could give me his classic disappointed face. "I met him as Elvis but knew he was an Elvis impersonator—except he said that he was the real Elvis. That couldn't be true, except it is—almost. Sort of. So Elvis became *the* Elvis, became sort of the real Elvis, became Patrick-Elvis. Clear?"

"Your thought processes are odd," said the guy who could only hold a conversation with strangers if he followed rules laid out by our murdered neighbor, Mrs. A.

"They are, aren't they?" Alex agreed with a great deal too much enthusiasm.

I met Alex's gaze in the rearview mirror and raised my

eyebrows. "You better stick to your best behavior for a while, Secretive Old Guy. So, Bradley, what about Patrick-Elvis?"

"Patrick Twombly is a forty-five-year-old man with two residences. The home he owns here was purchased about a month ago, and his previous residence in Minneapolis was purchased ten months previous. I couldn't find a prior residence for him."

"He must have gone to Minneapolis to complete the transition to his new face and been in the process of moving back to Austin with his new identity." Alex pulled into Patrick-Elvis's new neighborhood.

"Minneapolis? Not exactly the plastic surgery capital of America. I'd have guessed somewhere in California—or is that just silly?"

"No comment on California, but Minneapolis is a hub for enhanced living. Like Austin." Alex glanced at me. "And who said anything about plastic surgery?"

Before I could ask how in the world a guy could change his appearance without plastic surgery, I realized that Patrick-Elvis was a demigod. Altering his appearance might be one of his talents.

"What's a hub of enhanced living?" Bradley asked.

When Alex didn't jump on it, I said, "A place where there's a local enhanced government like the Society and, I guess, a lot of magical people."

"Yeah," Alex said, but he sounded distracted.

And he was driving like a little old lady.

I peered out my window at the quiet neighborhood. This was it. I'd been here just three days earlier. "Since you're not lost, you wanna tell me what has you driving like my Great-Aunt Lulu?

"Yes, this is definitely the correct street." Bradley pointed down the street and to the left.

Alex reached across the center console and pushed Bradley's arm down. "Don't point."

And he picked up the pace just a tick.

"What's going on?" I leaned forward in between the front seats and scanned the street for suspicious behavior.

"I don't know; something's off. I'm going to lap the block once, just to be sure."

"Are the guys saying you shouldn't stop?" I whispered, which was ridiculous, given that Bradley could obviously hear everything I said.

"No guys." Alex passed Patrick-Elvis's house. "None. Not on the entire street."

I looked behind us and ahead. It was a long street. "That seems weird. That is weird, isn't it?"

I'd always understood that spirits kinda hung around. That they were everywhere. And that wasn't even including the nasty ones that specifically hung around Alex.

"It might be odd." Alex stretched his neck. "Maybe. I don't know."

"What guys?" Bradley asked.

Alex and I both remained silent and refused to look at Bradley.

"I don't understand. What guys?"

Bradley wasn't exactly great at picking up on social cues.

"So, that's kind of a private thing between Alex and me." I tried to keep my tone light.

"Couples tell each other secrets, and sharing that information with other people is a violation of trust." Bradley nodded as he parroted back what must surely be one of Ms. A's pieces of social advice, likely intended to aid him in a future relationship with his own significant other. Mrs. A truly had been an optimist.

And Bradley thought that Alex and I were a couple. Awkward.

I scanned the surroundings and tried to be open to any messages the universe happened to be throwing my way—whether they were precognitive hints or a sense of unease that might indicate another hidden message. But I got nothing.

And then Alex pulled into Patrick-Elvis's driveway, still looking tense.

Too bad he couldn't give me a hint without tipping off Bradley about his spirit pest problem. Looked like we were going in blind.

11

VICIOUS VIBES

I harnessed Boone and got ready to jog behind him as he started his hunt for stinky bad-guy smells. But he just stood there.

"Your dog is broken." Bradley looked underwhelmed by Boone.

I frowned back at him, and in a quiet voice said, "He's not broken. And that's not very nice. He can understand you."

Bradley examined Boone. "He's a dog. He doesn't speak English."

Boone, who had been standing very still with his nose lifted slightly, turned to Bradley and woofed once.

Bradley jumped in surprise at the deep, vibrating pulse of sound that Boone produced.

I grinned and barely managed not to say, "So there." My dog was *not* broken.

Alex had already moved to the front door and was whispering, "Open the lock," as Bradley and I bickered over Boone. I turned back to my super-awesome, very-not-broken, sniffer hound and said, "Find some bad-guy smells."

Boone turned to the house and, nose inches from the ground, started his search. He moved with deliberation, nowhere near as quickly as he had at Akira's house.

Alex stood at the front door, waiting. He scanned the length of the street and said, "I know the scent is older, but it might be good for us to be inside sooner than later. It was hard enough to explain Boone working at Akira's house—and Patrick doesn't have any kids who might doing a class project. Not to mention this neighborhood looks more uptight."

"A class project? How did you get that to fly with Michelle gone?" But then, Alex could be very charming when he occasionally tried, and there had been several female neighbors... "Never mind."

After a few nervous minutes with me scanning the street for the curious—or flashing red and blue lights—I said, "Boone, any chance we can catch the rest of the exterior on the way out?"

He stopped snuffling the bushes, lifted his head just enough to catch my eye, then went back to snuffling.

Boone-ese for: "Stop your complaining, lady."

Since I didn't want to mess with Boone's sniffing mojo, I waited and watched. And almost hyperventilated.

There was a complex methodology to his searching. He was purposeful and intent, and he knew way more about finding bad-guy stink than I did. Thank goodness, because...ewwww.

Finally, Boone abandoned the bush next to the front door and then made a beeline for Alex. Instead of opening the door—which was what I would have done—Alex waited until Boone examined all the corners and crevices. When Boone finished, he rocked back on his haunches and sat in front of the door—and only then did Alex open it.

Mental note: doorways were magically delicious to my hound's keen nose. I gave Alex a curious look. How did he know that?

And how annoying was it that I didn't?

Once we were all inside, I removed Boone's leash, and the three of us followed him through the lower level of the house. It was much larger than Akira's.

When we'd finished most of the second floor, my nerves were about shot. Not finding anything was proving more stressful than the nasty message in the Mori's living room. I tried to shake off the feeling, and asked Bradley, "Does Patrick-Elvis live alone?"

"I found no evidence of a roommate or girlfriend or boyfriend or children."

"That's a yes, then," I said.

"Unless there's a captive hidden in the attic or under a bed."

Bradley's deadpan delivery gave me pause, but then I realized... "Bradley, did you just make a joke?"

"No. Too much late night television."

Which made me giggle. I couldn't help it, even with the weight of Akira's disappearance—and what was looking to be Patrick-Elvis's absence—hanging over me.

Alex didn't share my humor, and Bradley obviously thought I'd gone around the bend.

I shook my head, and I couldn't keep out the grumpy note when I said, "Never mind. It's not funny if I have to explain."

While time had seemed to drag, we'd almost covered the entire house. And there had been nothing of note in the spacious four-bedroom house. Nothing except a lot of near-OCD tidiness. "Did you get any weird vibes?" I asked Alex.

"Beyond your inappropriate laughter?" Alex paused,

then said, "There's still an eerie silence from the guys. And I'm tired." He rubbed the back of his neck. "More tired than I should be."

"That's odd." And bad. I understood why Alex might be both emotionally and physically wiped—we'd had a spectacularly full week—but he could gauge better than most if he was more tired than he should be.

Something hinky was up with the house.

Alex glanced at Bradley then back at me. I took the hint, sealed my lips, and followed Boone through the final upstairs bedroom.

As I watched Boone sniff his way back to the stairs, I started to worry about exactly how tired Alex might be.

A particularly nasty variety of spirit critters cropped up when Alex was tired—which he'd just admitted to. But also when he was sick or injured or stressed...or, really, any time he was having a bad day. Yeah, I needed to find out more about those things. And maybe why I could sometimes see and even touch them—but usually not.

As we walked down the stairs, still following Boone's lead, I stared at Alex's back. The T-shirt he wore hugged his broad shoulders, but covered the tattoos I knew were hidden there. Much as I squinted, changed angles, and concentrated, I didn't see even a hint of the misty green film that indicated a spirit of some kind was present in, near, or around him.

When Alex got to the bottom of the stairs, he looked over his shoulder at me. "You're staring a hole in my back. Quit it."

"Sorry." I gave him a sheepish look, but could he really blame me? We weren't that far out from a nasty demon possession.

He turned back to watch Boone, leaving me to feel guilt on top of all the anxiety that was cranking through my body.

There were some foul spirits tied to Alex with archaic and very bad magic. Apart from the nasty spirit critters that harassed Alex, there was another, more innocuous version running around—and they were the useful ones. Except those little, innocuous, useful spirit critters *weren't* running around. Not near Patrick-Elvis's house.

And then there were the tattoos. From Alex's behavior, he had to be ashamed of them, making it more likely they played some role in his possession.

I peeked at Alex's arms as discreetly as I could. Just in case his freaky wizard radar was on extra-sensitive. Not even a tiny hint of ink. I'd only seen him bare-chested on two occasions: once when I'd woken him in his office, and he'd thrown a shirt on as quickly as he could. And a second time when I'd been too drained by a near-death experience to notice much...about the tats. His chest I might have noticed. Lean, nice muscle definition, surprisingly broad shoulders. It made sense he looked more swimmer than football player, since he was a cardio and combat training kinda guy, and not into lifting weights.

And how weird was it that I knew that much about him? Not his age...but his workout schedule.

Ugh. So not okay that I found him drool-worthy barechested. Not since I'd found out he was old. Really old. Should-be-desiccated-and-buried-in-the-dirt old. I almost tripped.

Fast as a wink, Alex was next to me and steadied me with a hand under my elbow. He gave me an odd look.

"What?" I tried not to sound defensive, as if I'd not been picturing him half-naked then burying him prematurely in my mind.

Alex raised an eyebrow. "You're blushing."

"I'm not." I tried to sound calm and get rid of the blush that was warming my face, but it just got worse. "Well, now I am. Thanks for that."

Bradley said, "Boone didn't find anything."

Boone stopped the lazy circle he was making in the living room, turned to Bradley, and leveled him with a doggy stare that spoke volumes.

I decided to translate, just to be sure there was no doubt. "Boone disagrees...emphatically."

Bradley stood awkwardly in the middle of the room, looking like a kid who didn't get picked for the team. "I really don't understand how a dog speaks English."

"Bradley, are you telling me that you have no problem with me and Wembley being vampires, with Alex using magic to unlock the front door, with Elvis being sort of alive again...but a magic dog is weird to you?"

He considered my question, blinked, then said, "Yes."

"Um, 'kay." Because what did I say to that? I turned my attention to the poor, beleaguered hound. "Ignore him, Boone-dog. First things first. Is the owner of the house—that's Patrick-Elvis—the guy who nabbed Akira?"

Liquid brown eyes stared calmly back at me.

"Thank goodness," I said. Then I saw Bradley's confused look. "I mean, not good that he's gone and maybe nabbed. But now we know that he didn't do the nabbing, right?"

"Now we have some evidence that he didn't do the nabbing," Alex said.

I slipped him a squinty look then asked Boone, "Any signs of the bad guy from Akira's place?"

Boone's tail thumped, but with less enthusiasm than I might have hoped.

"You don't know who he is, do you?"

Boone groaned, and his wrinkly face drooped.

I hugged his big head against my leg and rubbed his ears. "You're doing great, buddy. You're giving us case-breaking, vital information. Isn't he, guys?"

Bradley was distracted by a painting on the wall and didn't respond, but Alex gave me an impatient look. "He's not a kid. He's a working dog."

I covered Boone's ears. "With feelings."

"Right." Alex turned to Boone and asked in a matter-of-fact tone, "Did you pick up any scents present on the scene at Akira and Michelle's house?"

That produced a very enthusiastic response; Boone's tail pounded on the floor in agreement.

"Uh-oh," I said. "Looks like we've found a second victim."

Alex rubbed his neck. "All we know is that there's a connection. He could have some type of relationship with Akira's attacker."

"Really? How likely do you think that is, Bradley?"

But he was still busy examining the painting on the wall. "This looks expensive."

Alex glanced at the picture. "Yeah, original and technically doesn't exist. Forget you saw it."

"Oh. I can do that." Bradley stepped away from it and turned back to us. No arguments or confusion. He was getting better at this whole "secret society with crazy secrets" thing. "Can your dog tell time? How long it's been since Patrick was here, for example?"

I did a little math and then asked, "Has Patrick-Elvis been here in the last three days?"

Boone lay down.

"Four days?" Alex asked.

Boone hopped up and wagged his tail.

Four days. That was when I'd seen Patrick-Elvis at the police station, dealing with his outstanding traffic ticket. "Come on, guys. He's been kidnapped." I sighed. "Or worse. You know it."

"Or he's hiding out for some other nefarious purpose," Bradley said.

"I thought you liked this guy?" I took off Boone's harness and attached his leash to his collar.

Red fur—and maybe a little bloodhound spit—flew as Boone gave a full-body shake. When he was done shedding on Patrick-Elvis's pristine and probably very expensive oriental area rug, he tugged on his leash.

As I followed him to the door, I looked over my shoulder.

"I admire his work." Bradley glanced at the painting. "But where there's evidence of one illegal act, it's easy to imagine more."

Harboring black market artwork was one thing—if that painting was even of shady origins—but kidnapping or worse was something else entirely. Boone pulled me to the door. Either he was done here...or he had to pee.

"I'm just worried that we'll miss the real bad guy because some other victim is under suspicion." I reached to open the door but stopped short of touching the door handle. "If something terrible has happened to him, how do we keep the cops out of it? There's bloodhound hair and our prints all over this place."

Bradley's eyes widened.

"Doesn't feel so good when the suspicion falls on you, does it?"

Alex nudged me aside and opened the door. "We make sure the police never become involved. We handle this ourselves, whatever happens." Alex stepped aside to let

Bradley and me through the door. "And worst case, we get Star to come in and wipe the place."

Bradley shook his head. "That doesn't seem right."

And I could see his point—I just didn't agree with him. I'd belonged to the Society long enough to know that it was best we policed our own. The alternatives were...unpalatable.

As we drove away from Patrick-Elvis's, my mood lightened noticeably. And when Alex turned out of the neighborhood, I wanted to sigh in relief—which was just weird. "Anyone else feel suddenly a lot happier?"

Bradley said, "No," as Alex said, "Yes, definitely."

Looking between the two men, I had to say, it was an easy win on who I'd trust with picking up on wicked vibes. "Sorry, Bradley, but I might go with Alex on this one. What are you thinking?"

Alex shifted uneasily in the driver's seat.

I groaned in frustration. "Bradley, you're awesome at secrets, right?"

Without hesitation, Bradley said, "Yes. I know all sorts of secrets about Mrs. A. And I have a contract with the Society to keep a secret. But I don't need a contract to keep a secret. My word is my bond." The last was clearly parroted Mrs. A advice. Actually, no, that sounded more like late night television.

"See, Alex? Totally trustworthy. Mrs. A was an excellent judge of character. If Mrs. A trusted Bradley..." I gave him a prodding look in the rearview mirror.

"It's not that big of a deal," Alex said, addressing the statement to Bradley. "But I'd rather it not be something you talked about."

"Okay. But we'll call it a secret, because that's what you really mean."

I had to swallow a laugh at Bradley's response. Especially since I doubted Alex found it funny.

"Right. Fine." Alex rubbed the back of his neck. "So the *secret* is that I can see spirits."

"Ghosts?" Bradley sounded fascinated—and not the least bit skeptical.

I glanced at Boone, the impossibly magical dog, but he didn't seem to take offense at the readiness with which Bradley accepted ghosts.

"I can see ghosts, but they're not very common. Spirits were never human; they're something else entirely. As are elementals—and demons."

"And you can see all of those?" No doubt about it, Bradley was fascinated.

I could see my ninja status slipping. It looked like Alex might be Bradley's new favorite crime fighter. Ah, well, no surprise there. Alex was pretty cool, with his sword-wielding awesomeness and wizardly magic.

I stopped at that thought. "Exactly what else can a wizard do, Alex?"

There was a beat of silence, then Alex said, "Lesser spirits are usually all around. Not interfering, not participating on this plane of existence, but everywhere. Patrick's street and the surrounding streets, however, were empty of spirits."

Not like I could call him out on avoiding my question. It had been a little low to ask, but I'd lay the blame on my post-transformation lack of impulse control. I'd actually been doing pretty well, so one little slip wasn't terrible. And a chance to learn about Alex's powers had been too juicy to pass up.

"Wait, several streets were empty of spirits? That's odd," I said.

Alex nodded. "And then combine that with the weighty feeling surrounding the place—not that you guys seemed to notice." He rolled his shoulders. "I'm guessing some bad magic tainted the area."

"Ah, like what we were talking about before, where something that's happened leaves an imprint on the place. And I did notice. Sort of. When I came here before to check the house out, it was discouraging to find nothing. *Very* discouraging." I'd gone straight home, punched a pillow, cuddled with Boone, and then taken a nap. "It's possible I murdered a pillow when I got home."

Alex snorted but quickly schooled his features into a bland expression and said, "Sorry."

Killing pillows was all fun and games until someone had to clean up the feathers. Since that someone had been me, I was less amused.

I considered the size of the small neighborhood. "Whoa —are you saying this tainted magic polluted the whole neighborhood? Because that's a lot of space."

"Yeah," Alex said with no lingering traces of amusement. "We're talking about large quantities of magic. Consider as well that one side of the neighborhood is bordered by a creek. Since running water can impact how magic spreads, it's possible the creek limited the spread."

"Can I go home now?" Bradley's non-sequitur didn't seem to take Alex by surprise.

"No." Lord love the man, that was all he said. Wise move, given that we'd already used the only truly enticing carrot we had: access to Patrick-Elvis's home.

I pursed my lips. I couldn't blame Bradley for wanting to scamper; we were discussing dangerous levels of magic. And the house had been disappointing when considered from the perspective of a rabid (stalkerish) Elvis fan. No personal items—no personalization—in Patrick-Elvis's house at all.

"Besides," I said, "you need to stick around for our new mystery: what chased the spirits out of the area?"

Alex's face tightened, then he said, "I'm pretty sure I know what left its mark on the area and probably also chased away the spirits."

I leaned forward, in between the front seats.

Alex elbowed me back. "Put your seatbelt on."

I ignored him but stayed out of elbow range. "Don't leave me hanging—what did this? What chased away all the spirits?"

Alex ran a hand through his hair. "At a guess...voodoo."

12

PC MAGIC

Alex hadn't budged for five miles: not a word about what voodoo was or why he thought voodoo was involved.

"I really don't understand why it's such a problem to share a little information. I'm just going to make my own assumptions, and they're likely wrong." Especially since all that came to my mind were the little dolls with the pins you stick in them—but I kept that to myself.

"Voodoo is a religious practice found primarily in Caribbean areas," Bradley recited as if he was reading from a dictionary or some kind of wiki.

I peeked over his shoulder, but his phone wasn't on. He frowned and inched away from me like I had cooties.

"Seatbelt, Mallory," Alex said. "You do remember asking me at some point whether a car crash would kill you like a normal person?"

Not only did I remember, I also recalled his answer including some level of uncertainty. Hm. I sat back in my seat and buckled up. "Where are we going? Because we're obviously not taking Bradley home." I kicked Bradley's seat

—and felt all of eight doing it—but he deserved it. I do *not* have cooties. Vampirism isn't contagious, not in that way. Besides, I hugged him all the time.

Alex made a sound that was suspiciously similar to a growl. "Buda."

And I knew only one person who lived in Buda: Star. "So voodoo is a kind of witchcraft?"

"Voodoo is a lot of different things. Bradley's right, of course; it has a religious and cultural side. That's not the kind I'm talking about. Voodoo is also slang for bad magic, black magic, out-of-control or unauthorized magic."

Hm. That seemed kind of broad. But if accurate, then it was like the Society was saying some magic was politically correct and some wasn't. "Are you sure you know what voodoo is?" Since my question made a muscle in his jaw twitch that I could see all the way from the back seat, maybe it was a little rude.

"I'm sure," he whispered.

I looked at him again. He wasn't offended; he was troubled.

Then a tiny light went on in the back of my sluggish brain. Those tattoos on Alex's body probably had something to do with what he was calling voodoo. Wembley had said as much; he just hadn't used the same words. He'd said archaic, dark magic. Better not to mention those tats in front of Bradley. They were a secret I was certain Alex wasn't willing to share.

"Will Patrick-Elvis's neighborhood ever be okay?" I asked. "I mean, not that they need spirits flitting around. But that nasty vibe is no treat."

The tension in Alex's shoulders eased. "Yeah. That's another reason we're visiting Star. I'm hoping she's available to cleanse the area sooner rather than later. I'm sure the effect will dissipate with time, but if we can save a few couples from unnecessary marital discord or some kids from undeserved punishments, all the better."

And there it was, one of the big reasons I called Alex friend. He was a decent guy. Of course, I'd never say it out loud, because he'd be embarrassed. Or deny it. And that was weird. In hundreds of years—literally centuries—he hadn't learned to take a compliment? The guy was an oddball.

But I couldn't comment on his thoughtfulness, I couldn't ask about his tats, and Bradley was hardly a conversational dynamo now that his backseat-driving chatter had died down. So I kept myself to myself...all the way to Buda. It was torture.

Forever later, I asked, "Are we almost there?"

"We're five minutes closer than the last time you asked." Alex caught my glance in the rearview mirror. His expression didn't match his words. He definitely looked amused and not irritated.

I shrugged.

"You act like a couple," Bradley said.

"What?" I snapped out the question before I could think about it. Alex grinned.

"You and Alex. You say you're not a couple, but you act like a couple." After a second, Bradley said, "A couple on television."

Right, because Bradley didn't actually have much access to real couples. Being the next best thing to a shut-in and all. Which made it easier to disregard his comment. Sure, I'd wondered if Alex and I might have been going on a *date* date for the Elvis thing. But that outing had clearly been a friend thing, more of an appointment-type date.

And now that I knew how ancient Alex was, did I even want to see him that way? He did have that accountant/bad-boy thing going for him, which, I couldn't lie to myself, I definitely found sexy. But that reminded me of my interior designer's comment about how Alex looked like a clean-cut, modern version of an old west sheriff. Where she got that... Weird. Add in his freakish effect on basically all women in a thirty-foot radius, and the only conclusion was that something fishy was going on.

"Do wizards have some kind of magical sex appeal?" And those words did indeed leave my lips. I closed my eyes, because I couldn't begin to imagine Alex's response—and didn't particularly want to witness it.

I cracked an eye and found him grinning. "What makes you ask?" And there it was, the smugness, the confidence, and the male ego of a guy who'd had a really long time to build them up to massive proportions.

"Forget I asked."

"We're here," Bradley said.

Which I'd missed amid my embarrassment. Stupid fritzy impulse control. Alex had parked around the backside of the building—where the bodies came in. "Yay! Let's go save some marriages and some little kids from being grounded."

And Alex laughed.

A mellow, relaxed sound that I didn't hear very often. And that sound—the sound of his amusement—erased my embarrassment. It made me wish he would laugh more often. Except for the small problem that a laughing Alex was one sexy beast.

I rolled down the backseat windows, wagged a finger at Boone, warning him to stay in the car, and hopped out. *Walk away, girl, just walk away.*

"Whoa. Slow down," Alex said as he jogged to catch up. "I didn't call ahead, just texted we were on the way. Star doesn't know why we're here."

I hadn't realized my admonishment to myself had resulted in me running—rather than walking—away. I looked over my shoulder to find Bradley in no particular hurry to join us, which brought me to a stop. "She doesn't bite, Bradley."

But his pace didn't increase, and I could only hope he didn't hear Alex whispering, "Much."

When he joined us, Bradley said, "She does, too." At my look of confusion, he added, "Bite. She bites, metaphorically. Star has a reputation."

I paused several feet from the back door, because we were not walking inside the woman's place of business as we discussed her.

The feeling that everyone knew more than me was driving me crazy. Especially since Bradley was hardly in the midst of enhanced living. Except he was...sort of, because of that darn app. "Was Star in the book? And your app?"

"Yes. Witch, class three." Bradley started to recite several names.

"No, that's okay. I don't need her aliases." I really, really didn't need to know anything about Star that she didn't specifically want me to know. Memory excision was a witch skill, and Star was a powerful witch. No thanks; I liked my brain just as it was, thank you.

Bradley fell silent and then looked longingly at the car; the poor guy just wanted to go home.

Alex started toward the door, but I stopped him with a hand on his arm. Because I couldn't do it; I couldn't rein in my nosiness. My curiosity nudged-shoved-threatened me, and it was impossible to ignore. This was the second time someone I knew had come up with a number classification. Wembley had been the other; he'd been labeled a class three vampire in Bradley's app.

So I asked, "Do we have any clue what that classification means?"

Bradley considered the question as if it was a new one. "Wembley, Cornelius, and Star are threes, and Alex is a four. There are more ones than fives—but I didn't recognize those names. I don't have sufficient data to be certain, but the higher numbers appear to be an indication of greater skill."

That didn't seem right. Alex had pesky spirit critters harassing him, and it wasn't like he could control them. He also didn't seem to have a bunch of really awesome magical talents. Like illusion—that was a pretty rocking enhancement, but Alex couldn't do that. Yeah, Bradley had his math wrong.

Except he probably didn't, because he was Bradley.

I looked at Alex, but he wouldn't meet my gaze.

I pointed a finger at him, something he couldn't miss, even in his peripheral vision. "You and I are going to have a chat, mister."

He shrugged. "Anytime—but not now. And Bradley? You're not supposed to have a copy of that app, so you might want to keep it low key that you've got the contents stored in your computer brain."

Bradley nodded slowly, his eyes wide. "I should wait in the car," he said as he headed that direction. If he'd considered it an option earlier, I'd bet we couldn't have gotten him out of the Jeep at all.

"Bradley." Alex waited for him to stop and turn then said, "She's mostly retired now. Barely does any magic at all."

"That's right!" I jumped on the bandwagon "And she has four kids. So she's basically a full-time mom."

Bradley gave me that disappointed look. "She's a mortician, so she can't be a full-time mom."

Said the guy who didn't have four kids...but I let it go. "The point is, she's not the same person today as whoever did those things you read about."

Later, Bradley and I would have to have a chat about what exactly was in that book he'd used to create the app. Because I hadn't realized there was more than a basic classification, enhancement type, and aliases included. Hopefully, no one else realized exactly how much information floated around inside Bradley's head. Or how good his recall was.

Bradley's expression was mulish. "People don't change that much."

"Shame on you," I said, and meant it. "Mrs. A wouldn't agree with that at all. If she did, she'd never have been friends with you or encouraged you to make other friends. Right?"

"Sometimes you're not very nice." But he turned away from the car and joined us. "If she hexes us, I'm blaming you."

I tried not to laugh—like Star would hex us. Then a hint of doubt niggled. I shot Alex a nervous look.

He just rolled his eyes and opened the door for me.

How a semi-retired witch ended up as a mortician, I couldn't guess. Although I supposed it made sense that anyone in the enhanced community would be less squeamish than the run-of-the-mill citizen. Chopping off heads in self-defense, hanging criminals, neck-biting for food; there was a lot of weirdness in the community. But it still seemed an odd choice.

"I thought you guys were going to pitch a tent and camp out there." Star didn't look up from her task when she addressed us. And that was particularly disconcerting, because she was busy prepping a guy for burial. Not to mention there was no indication of security cameras or other electronic surveillance visible, so how had she known?

Witches definitely had the best magic, whatever Alex said.

"They made me come," Bradley said, taking a step back from Star—and the corpse.

I snorted but regained my composure as quickly as I could. "Uh, hi, Star. Thanks again for your help with the whole murder thing."

She put aside the makeup palette she'd been holding and looked up. "No problem; I got paid."

"Sure, still, thank you."

She flashed me a smile—one of the few I'd seen from her—and said, "My pleasure." She pointed a finger at Alex as she walked over to a washbasin. "And you, shut it. I can be nice."

"I never said otherwise. So, I have a project for you." And Alex told her about the neighborhood and the odd feelings and the lack of spirits as she scrubbed her hands in the huge metal washbasin. Then he asked her if she could clear it.

"Usual fee, and I can't get to it until tonight after the kids are in bed."

Alex nodded his agreement. He'd haggle all day with Cornelius, but not Star. I wasn't sure why that was, or which was the more typical transactional scenario in the Society, but I'd definitely be giving that some thought in future.

Hands on her hips, Star said, "Now tell me why you're really here. We could have done that over the phone."

"I need you to verify a statement." Alex's answer was oddly ambiguous, as was his expression, so I looked at Star for some clue as to what he meant.

She was giving him a hard look.

After a moderately uncomfortable silence—for me; Star

seemed fine with it—Star finally pointed a finger at me and said, "Not if it's her." Alex shook his head, and then she said, "Three times the normal rate."

"Hey, Bradley," Alex said, "you're not broke, right?"

Bradley looked up with a faint look of horror. I hadn't realized, but he'd been inspecting a row of what looked like surgical tools.

I motioned for him to come stand by me. Since he immediately joined me, I guessed that vamp cooties weren't so bad as embalming implements.

"You have three grand for our friend here?" Alex asked.

"Why would I give a witch three thousand dollars?"

I tried not to wince.

Star snapped her fingers. "Watch the language, buddy. And it's four now, because I don't like you."

Alex closed his eyes. When they opened, he had a curiously blank expression on his face. Either his patience was wearing thin, or he was tamping down some serious amusement. "Bradley, would you like to go home and not have the Society bother you while we finish up this investigation?"

"Yes," Bradley replied with no hesitation.

"Is it worth three grand"—Alex flashed a glance at Star —"to you to not be bothered by the Society for a few days?"

That was appalling. Extortionate. Terrible. "No way is that—"

"Sure." Bradley pulled out his wallet. "Is a check okay?"

"Bradley. Don't you dare," I said.

"Why not? I want to go home. And I don't actually want my head messed with. *You* keep saying that could happen." He looked around for a pen, and Star handed him one from the pocket in her apron. He eyed it with some misgiving, but took it after only a brief hesitation. "That's what this is about, right? You guarantee my silence?"

"Yes," Star said, her hands folded primly in front of her.

"Does it hurt?" He was scribbling out that check for three grand like it was nothing.

"It depends." Bradley stopped writing and looked up at Star, so she explained. "If you're honest, it doesn't hurt. But some people think they're being honest when, in fact, they're lying to themselves. That hurts. A lot. And it's no picnic for me, either."

Bradley signed the check and handed it to her. "I'm not like that."

And I really didn't think he was. Star must have agreed, because she didn't dwell or try to prepare him for an unpleasant experience. She simply pocketed the check in her apron and then stretched out both hands, palms up.

With great reluctance, Bradley reached out his hands. She grasped them firmly, and asked, "Do you intend to reveal the secret of the Society's existence to humanity?"

"No," Bradley said in a flat tone. I couldn't tell if that was just Bradley being Bradley, or she'd magicked him.

Star continued to hold his hands for several seconds. Then she let them go. "You pass."

"That's it?" That was what I said. What I meant was: Three grand for *that*?

"Well, yes, and the signed affidavit I'll be submitting to the Society on Bradley's behalf." Star hesitated, then said to Bradley, "You're an okay kid."

Since Bradley was hardly a kid, her comment made me wonder how old *she* was. Age was definitely on my brain today. Also, what exactly had she seen when she'd looked inside his head that made her take a liking to Bradley? He was a lovely guy—but he'd grown on me over time. He wasn't exactly the immediately endearing type. But I managed to keep my lips sealed and whisper not a peep of either of those questions.

"What else you got for me?" Star asked Alex.

"You know me so well. If there's voodoo involved, I'd like protection. Just for Mallory and me. Bradley should be safely tucked away at home."

"Good idea. I have something that should work for you, Alex, with some modification to accommodate your particular issue." Star pursed her lips as she examined me. "But you..." She squinted and peered at me like I was a bug under a microscope. "You're new. And you're definitely odd. Let's have a look."

That was when I remembered her comment from a previous meeting. She'd said, vegan or no, that I was no fluffy bunny. At the time, I'd appreciated it. When a girl is surrounded by hyper-capable people, anything less than awesome felt like underachieving. Considering I was less than awesome in my vampiness, it had been nice for someone to recognize that I might have my own sharp edges.

"Mallory, are you coming?" Alex asked.

I glanced at the deceased gentleman on the prep table as I passed—and I could have sworn he smiled at me. "Coming!" I hollered as I picked up my pace.

13

THE CLOSET OF MAGIC

I hurried after Star, Alex, and Bradley through a set of double doors, trying to escape the creepy sensation of a dead guy watching me.

I arrived in time to see Star hand Bradley a silver charm hung from a thin leather strip. "Wear it until Alex and Mallory sort out this voodoo magic issue. And no charge."

Whoa. I must have missed something. No charge?

Bradley pulled the necklace over his head without comment.

Star leaned down to the lowest shelf and reached back into a corner. She pulled out a black velvet pouch then dumped the contents in her hand: a signet ring. She turned and presented it to Alex.

He had an odd look on his face when he accepted it. "Can I put it on, or do you need to make the adjustments first?"

"Go ahead."

He slipped the ring onto the pinkie finger of his left hand, and I could feel the tension as he waited for something to happen. But then Star grabbed his hand and held on tight. This was nothing like what she'd done with Bradley. She was gritting her teeth like she was in pain, and Alex's right hand was balled up tight.

I inched away without realizing it, but when I hit the doorframe, I stopped. Only then, when I couldn't move away, did I feel the force pushing me away—psychic, physical, magical? I wasn't sure.

"Done." Star's voice was clipped, and she was a little out of breath. She shooed us out of the supply closet, but then pointed at me. "Not you. You need to do a little shopping."

"Do I get to ask about the aura power wash?" I wasn't sure where that imagery came from, but after I said it, I decided it sounded right.

"You felt that?" Star asked, then frowned over my shoulder.

"I definitely felt that." I turned to see Alex dip his chin in a curt nod.

Star bit her lip—the first sign of indecision I'd ever seen her make. "Because of the bindings that cover Alex's body, I had to adjust the protection charm. Otherwise, the charm would be drained trying to protect him from his own magic. But that won't be an issue for you. Now come and choose."

I was feeling conflicted: glad not to have some bizarre force giving my aura a bath, but disappointed that Alex and Bradley got the royal treatment while I was all self-serve.

Star sighed. "Look, protection isn't cheap, and when someone else is picking up the bill, I know I wouldn't decline."

"Speaking of bills," Alex said, flashing the signet ring, "you better not be charging me for this."

And that was the first time I'd seen Alex complain about Star's rates, and enough to distract me from my charm-choosing.

There was a brief and very curious exchange between the two, and Star finally said to me, "I might have lifted that particular item in my younger days."

Alex's lips twitched. "From me."

More of Alex's very lengthy past, cropping up in the present—why was I not surprised?

Star looked unapologetic. "I knew it would come in handy someday, and look. It has." Her levity disappeared when she turned to me. "You want to be as well prepared as magically possible if you're going head to head with voodoo magic. Take the charm."

She was right. It wasn't like I was going to decline...I just didn't know where to start. "Fine already. But how do I decide?"

"You can start by having a look at what's available." Star stepped to the side, making room for me in the small space.

Wasn't she just full of commonsense and practical advice? I wrinkled my nose and dove in.

At first they looked like a mishmash of items: coins, trinkets, figurines, watches, compasses, and, of course, jewelry. They had one thing in common: the items were small enough to carry—some more easily than others, like Alex's ring and Bradley's necklace—but even the largest could be tucked into a medium-sized purse or messenger bag. Have magical protection, will travel, I guess.

"Okay, I really could use some guidance here, because nothing is jumping out and biting me on the nose." As I spoke, I placed my hand on one of the shelves. My fingers started to warm, first with a pinching tingle, as if my digits were cold-numbed and thawing, and then they flooded with warmth.

If I'd just come inside from a frigid winter day, it

wouldn't mean a thing. But Texas in October was hardly icy cold.

I dropped down to my knees and pulled out the bin closest to my hand—and there it was, right on top: a rose-pink velvet choker with rhinestones. Not my usual style, but calling to me nonetheless.

I reached for it, and the moment my fingers brushed against it I felt a warmth wrap around me. Like being snuggled in a down comforter on a cold night, or drinking hot tea when you're so cold you can feel it in your bones. Like comfort and love and home, all wrapped together. Then the feeling faded to the background.

I lifted it so that Star could see it. "This one."

"Well, that's gonna cost you a fortune," Star said to Alex. Alex shrugged, and Star turned back to me with an outstretched hand. "I can put it on for you, but you'll have to remove it yourself whenever you decide to take it off."

Handing it over, I wasn't sure what I expected. I lifted my hair away from my neck and turned my back to Star. She briskly clasped it around my neck and absolutely nothing happened. She didn't linger, or grasp my hand like she did with Alex. And I certainly didn't have the feeling that my aura was being cleansed with an electric toothbrush.

I turned back around with a smile. "I've never been much of a rhinestones kinda gal, but it feels right."

"Those aren't..." Star blinked, her gaze at a point over my shoulder. "Ah, those aren't gaudy like most rhinestones. I think it's a very attractive, tasteful piece. It suits you. How does it feel?"

"Nice. Chocolate chip cookies and baking bread nice."

Star gave me a wide, genuine smile. "Perfect." Turning to Alex, she said, "You, I'll be billing. For the necklace, not the ring."

"Thank you." Sarcasm was thick in his voice. "I'd prefer not to pay for the recovery of my own stolen property."

"I've invested some serious magic in that object." She lifted her chin. "You're welcome."

Bradley raised his hand, something I thought he'd stopped doing.

"You don't have to raise your hand, Bradley," I said. "Remember, we talked about that?"

"Okay, but can we leave now? I'd like to go home."

I turned to Alex for an answer, and I caught him checking me out. Not in the oh-you're-so-hot-way. At least, I didn't think it was that way. I shot him a curious look.

"The necklace does suit you." Alex said. "Even in jeans and a T-shirt, it works."

My hand crept up my neck, and I rubbed the soft velvet.

"Home?" At least Bradley managed to ask without raising his hand.

"Yeah, I think it's safe for you to camp out in your condo now. It would be hard for one of Cornelius's witches to mess with your memory while you're wearing a protection charm." Alex gave Bradley a hard look. "Don't take it off."

I waved a goodbye to Star and then waited until we'd passed by the dead guy on the prep table and were walking outside before I said to Alex, "Aren't you one of Cornelius's goons?" I asked.

"Not when it comes to memory wipes, I'm not." Alex's voice was grim.

Good to know I could count on Alex to have both my back and my brain.

14

DEMEANING THE BEAN

A lex, Bradley, and I traveled in silence for most of the ride home. Bradley was done with humanity for the day, maybe the week. Alex probably figured if he kept his mouth shut, he wouldn't precipitate any undesirable questions. I just needed a little time to consider the plan. Or at least *a* plan.

I didn't want to get ditched, and I knew I was getting dropped at home before Bradley. But if I came up with our next strategic step, maybe it would be harder for Alex to leave me in the dust.

I'd come up with a decent set of questions by the time we got back to Austin. And while questions were hardly a plan, asking them was one step closer. "I think there might be other victims. Is there any way to track them down?"

"How would you propose we go about finding additional victims?" Alex asked. When his question was met with complete silence, he shook his head. "No one has been reported missing other than Akira by her daughter. If Patrick-Elvis...Patrick *Twombly* was abducted, it was before Akira. So he could have been a higher-priority target."

"You think if we can figure out why our kidnapper is snatching people, we can figure out who his other targets might be. We check in with the likely candidates—maybe drop a word of warning in their ears—and build a list of victims based upon those we can't reach."

"Yep," Alex said.

"Well, nuts. How do we get a pattern out of two events?" This was a little depressing, but I bit my tongue for joining the naysayer crowd. I much preferred the cheerleader role.

"Two is insufficient to identify a pattern, but you can trace the commonalities." Bradley turned around in his seat. "Paranormal—or enhanced, if you prefer—located within Austin city limits, members of the Society, and mentioned in my app. I'm sure there are many more, but those are the ones that come to mind."

"Wait a minute." Alex's face took on a grim cast. "Patrick and Akira do share another commonality: they're both unique members of the enhanced community."

I wasn't sure why that particular bit of information was bothersome to Alex, because it made me happy as a clam. "It's a relief to find out that there aren't a bunch of gods cruising around in Austin."

"I don't understand," Bradley said.

Uh-oh. What were the chances that Bradley's stalker brain would implode if I told him his hero was a demigod, worshipped into existence by rabid fans not unlike Bradley himself? I wasn't really a statistics kinda gal; give me geometry any day. I crossed my fingers. "So, Bradley, I have some news about Patrick-Elvis." And I proceeded to explain the concept of demigods.

When I was finished, Bradley said, "Cool."

That was it: just "cool."

"And yet Boone understanding English is shockingly

unlikely?" I asked. Boone was gonna get a complex.

"Boone's a dog."

A serious complex. I groaned in frustration. Boone nudged my hand with his wet nose, so I reached over to pet him—and I'd swear the hound was laughing at me.

"About Michelle," Alex said, "she didn't know of anyone who might want to harm her mother, hadn't noticed her mom acting oddly recently or more stressed than usual. And an important point about Michelle: she's not kitsune. Not yet."

"So if Michelle isn't yet fully kitsune, does that mean Akira is the only one in the area?" I asked.

"Probably in the state, definitely in the Austin area."

Bradley perked up. "How many demigods are in the Austin area?"

"Including Patrick?" Alex asked. "One."

I rubbed Boone's ears as I considered the implications. "Still, like Bradley said before, two isn't enough for a pattern."

"Yeah." Alex met my gaze in the rearview mirror. "Don't take that choker off."

I wrinkled my nose. "I do occasionally shower."

"Take a bath instead. Besides, I'm sure Star has some sort of preservation spell protecting the velvet. Protection charms are meant to be worn regularly."

Bradley was watching us both closely now, and he raised his hand.

I didn't bother to comment, just said, "Yes, Bradley?"

"You're unique. He's worried."

I blinked, swallowed, and inhaled a slow breath. I was a possible target. Alex was worried I'd be nabbed.

I didn't dwell on the thought that it had taken Bradley— a guy who was less than perceptive when it came to social cues—to point this out to me. I was way too busy freaking out that I might have a target on my back.

When Alex pulled into my driveway, I couldn't think about anything else. "Maybe you can have Anton check in on Ralph? Just to make sure he doesn't have anything to do with this." He'd always seemed a long shot, but when the skin on the back of my neck prickled—and I might be on a target list—it was best to investigate *all* leads.

"I'll speak with him." He hesitated with his hand on the car door handle. "He found the app contractor."

Something was off about the way he said it.

"When did that happen?" I asked.

"A while ago. The guy was dead. It wasn't necessarily tied to Society business, and, up till now, I'd have said that was a good outcome." Alex turned around in his seat. "We didn't do it, and it made the situation much simpler."

"Well, that's awesome that some guy's death was convenient for the Society. What were you thinking, not telling me?" I asked. Firmly. Maybe loudly.

Bradley ducked his head. I took a calming breath. Yelling wasn't helping anyone.

"I was thinking you didn't need the added stress when it was a resolved issue," Alex said. "Except the book wasn't recovered."

"And now it's possible that either the app or the book are being used to target enhanced Society members." I felt a guilty surge of relief, because I wasn't in the book. "Why are you telling me now?"

Alex shot Bradley a look. "Because Bradley and I are going to brainstorm on possible victims on the drive back to his place."

And what he told Bradley, Bradley would tell me—unless it became a part of the great vault of secrets my sidekick was holding. I held out my hand for my keys. "Consider sharing what you guys come up with."

Alex promised he would, and he looked just contrite enough for me to believe him.

I mumbled a thank you for my beautiful protection charm, accepted my keys, and said goodbye. I even let Boone out without attaching his leash. I stumbled zombie-like to my front door and walked inside, distracted by the news of yet another death. Maybe related? Maybe not?

Boone nudged past me and headed straight for the kitchen.

"Wembley!"

"No need to yell, heathen, I'm in the kitchen. With company."

Odd. We never had visitors. Contractors and designers, but not visitors who stopped by. My curiosity was piqued. Maybe Wembley was making nice with the neighbors. I'd only chatted with a few of them so far, and definitely hadn't had anyone over for coffee and cookies.

I entered the kitchen and stumbled to a halt.

Or maybe the police had come calling. Again.

"Detective Ruiz." I sat down at the kitchen table where Detective Ruiz was situated with, yes, a coffee and a plate of cookies.

"The detective came by to apologize. Coffee?" Wembley asked.

"Oh, I can get it myself." I started to stand up, but Wembley motioned for me to stay seated and went to fetch me a cup. "So, detective, do I need to call my attorney?"

Detective Ruiz leaned forward. "That's up to you, but this is hardly an official visit. I've been warned off. You seem to have some well-connected friends."

Which probably made me look all the more suspicious.

The detective certainly didn't look convinced of my innocence.

"I don't really understand why I'm in your sights. I haven't done anything." I gave him a hard look. "And this isn't sounding like an apology."

"Ms. Andrews, I'd like to apologize for doing my job and trying to find the man who killed eleven women. I'd also like to apologize for pursuing the one solid lead I have." He leaned back in his chair.

"I see."

"Do you? Because I don't. I don't see how you can stand by while a predator is targeting and killing single professional women—not so different from you—and do nothing. You need to tell me what you know." And this time it was him giving *me* the hard look. "I know that you have information."

I had to admire the guy's righteous sense of justice—mostly because I'd felt exactly the same way about the Society's lack of interest or cooperation in pursuing the same villain. But I wasn't deserving of his criticism, and my progenitor was deader than dead. Color me annoyed.

If only there was some legit, not-gonna-get-me-disciplined-by-the-Society way to convey my progenitor's status to the overzealous detective... Nope. Nothing came to mind. Worse than nothing, all of my hypothetical options ended up with me doing time.

Wembley returned with a cup of coffee for me. Good thing, because I didn't see any way around the Society's no-reveal clause and that was making this whole situation rather pleasant. Maybe even putting a crimp in my happy. I took a sip and had to swallow a moan of pure, blissful pleasure. "What did you do to my coffee? It's even better than usual."

Wembley gave me a smug look. "Cinnamon."

I wrapped my hands around the mug and savored my second sip. "I think I might be in love."

"That's a lot of enthusiasm for a bunch of boiled beans."

Wembley and I turned to the detective with mirror expressions of horror.

"Don't demean the bean, man." The high that Wembley got from coffee might mean he couldn't drink much of it, but that certainly didn't decrease his admiration.

I just shook my head. There was simply no response to such disrespect.

"Sorry." Ruiz lifted his mug and took a drink. "It's really good."

"Yes, well, you've managed to deliver the worst apology ever, and implied I'm in either in cahoots with a serial killer or don't want him caught. Pardon me for saying I don't really care if you enjoy your coffee or not."

The detective stood up, reached into his back pocket, and pulled out his wallet. He retrieved a business card, placed it on the table, and tapped it. "Just in case you change your mind."

"There's simply nothing to say." I stood up. "I'll walk you out. I need to get something out of the car anyway."

Mostly I wanted to see his car, because I didn't want him sneaking up on me again.

I opened the door for him and followed him out, tugging it shut behind me so Boone didn't cruise into the yard and start acting in an oddly un-doglike manner.

I scanned the street and made a guess at the detective's car. "That's your truck?"

"Nope, the Prius." He pointed to a silver car parked in front of my neighbor's house.

I checked to make sure he wasn't pulling my leg, and

from his expression, I didn't think he was.

"And that's what I always drive. Unlike your boyfriend, I don't own a used car dealership."

I started to protest that Alex wasn't my boyfriend, then I realized what he'd said. I walked past my Jeep and followed him out to the street. "How do you know that Alex owns a car dealership?"

"Seriously? I'm a detective, and I'm not crap at my job." He hesitated when he reached his car, then said, "Except for showing up on your doorstep today. But the next time I'm here, it will be in a much more official capacity—and not driving my personal car."

Was I that obvious with my avoid-the-detective plan? I waved a hand dismissively. "I won't rat you out, not unless you do something shady and deserving of being ratted out. I get it, wanting to catch this guy. I really do. I just can't help you."

"You won't help. There's a difference."

I sighed. This again. If he was a little less cute and a little less right, I'd be livid. But he was more than cute and spot on.

The truck I'd guessed was Detective Ruiz's was headed toward us, driving on the wrong side of the road. And in front of a cop, no less. The guy might as well yell, *Hey, I'm drunk!*

But then I had a nasty, creepy feeling.

I didn't know why, but I grabbed the detective's arm. It was more a reflex than a choice, and I did it with the lightning speed that occasionally kicked in when I was adrenaline-dumping like crazy. My fingers clasped tightly around his forearm.

And that was when it hit us. A wave, a pulse, a blast? I wasn't sure...

15

AN UNKNOWABLE NASTY

A sharp pain in my temple jogged me awake. The hard metal under my hip and my cheek, the vibration and sway of the floor under me, and street noises—I was in a car...a truck...the bed of a truck. As the fog cleared from my head, I realized I was in trouble.

Moving first my hands, then my legs, I found that I wasn't bound. The blanket covering me crinkled as I investigated—probably a tarp. That seemed odd.

And if I was in the bed of a truck, my bet was on the truck that had driven by when I'd been zapped. I'd bet serious cash on it.

I stretched out my hand to the right, searching for some sense of orientation—maybe the edges of the truck bed—and found nothing. I stretched my hand out to my left and bumped up against the warm flesh of another person. I swallowed a scream as a wave of panic washed through me.

Alex and I were having a chat. Assuming I survived. Which I totally would. Even if I couldn't breathe. Thinking about reaming Alex for telling me vamps couldn't have panic attacks when I clearly was having a panic attack helped me breathe better. There was some irony for a girl.

And that was when I realized that the warm body next to me had to be Detective Ruiz. He'd been right next to me when I was zapped. I'd grabbed the guy, so I'd been holding on to him while zapped.

I weighed how sure I was—because poking some strange body stashed next to me under the cover of tarp-induced darkness in the back of a truck fell into the risky category any which way I looked at it. Better to hold off if I wasn't pretty sure.

As I debated Ruiz or not Ruiz, I heard the bark of a dog. I knew that dog: high-pitched, ear-piercing, and an exact match for the pup right behind my house. We were still in my neighborhood. I couldn't believe my luck. Slow speeds, stop signs, and familiar territory.

"Ruiz." I shoved against the person I really, truly, desperately hoped was Detective Ruiz. Preferably an alive Detective Ruiz.

I shuddered. He could be dead. Newly dead bodies were still warm. Ick. Ickickcick.

The truck was slowing down.

Nuts. Touch the dead guy in hopes he was still alive or wake the living guy in hopes he was Ruiz. So many bad outcomes there.

I steeled myself and shoved harder. The body shifted—because I'd shoved so hard? Because he'd moved?

And then it moaned. Ruiz's moan? Some other dude's?

Good grief. Where were my ladyballs?

I shoved hard and said, "Wake up, Ruiz." Because it was Ruiz. The other alternative was not so good, and I was keeping my danged happy alive and well, even if I was kidnapped.

"What the— Ow." Relief washed through me. Such a beautiful sound. Not feelings I would have predicted back when the guy was arresting me.

"We're in the bed of a truck. A bad guy's truck." The truck rolled to a stop as I explained, but it immediately pulled forward again.

"What?" Ruiz sounded out of it.

"Wakey, wakey. We're in trouble." I started groping Ruiz to see if maybe he'd been tied up, even if I hadn't.

"Hey, watch it. That's my... Just watch it, Andrews." His voice sounded much clearer.

"I was checking to see if you were tied up."

"Not tied. Where are we? What happened?"

No time for the whole "magically zapped" explanation, so I gave the abbreviated version. "We're still in my neighborhood. Not sure of the details, but we need to get out when it stops."

I inched to the back of the truck. But we'd missed yet another opportunity; the truck was moving again at a good clip.

"Do you know where we are?" Detective Ruiz's voice had finally lost the dazed quality, and he sounded all sorts of pissed off.

"Still in my neighborhood. I'm not sure where, but there's only two choices. We've either got a roundabout coming or a stop sign."

He crawled to the back with more stealth than me. Once again, my vampiness was underwhelming. Nothing new there. When he reached my side, he asked, "Did you see any weapons?"

"Are you kidding? I didn't see anything—just woke up in the back of a truck."

He was pressed close next to me, so I could feel him

reaching out to test the tailgate. I heard a click and he said, "All right. Once we slow down, I'll lower the tailgate as quietly as I can. Don't go until I tell you. If the truck's moving too fast, we'll be picking up your brain matter off the road later."

"Thanks for that."

"I'm serious." His voice was low and intense. "If there are no obstacles, you want to go to the right where there's no oncoming traffic—and hopefully some grass. Tuck and roll. You got it?"

We were slowing down.

"Do you have it? Tuck and roll, to the right if it's clear."

"I've got it." And the truck stopped.

Ruiz lowered the tailgate and shifted the tarp aside. We were still at a full stop. Thank the Lord for that, because I did *not* have it with the tucking and the rolling. I hopped out as quickly as I could and crouched low. Ruiz jumped out right after me—except he was smart enough to immediately check the license plate. He read the letters aloud five times. Then he made a mnemonic. In basically two seconds. While crouched behind a quickly departing kidnapper vehicle. Not bad.

"Come on. Let's go," he said as the truck turned right. And, bold as you please, he walked up the nearest driveway.

"I can't believe he didn't see us." The truck had disappeared around the turn, and still I was sure whoever was driving it was coming back for us.

"We were supposed to be knocked out, or he would have tied us up. And a lot of people don't check their rearview mirror as often as they should—even nervous kidnapper types."

I squinted at him as he briskly knocked on the front door.

He glanced at me and said, "They don't."

Detective Ruiz asked the woman who answered the door if he might please use her phone, as there had been an accident.

And that was how I ended up in Stella's kitchen, waiting for Wembley to come get me.

Stella, the lovely lady who'd answered the door, said, "I just can't believe it, right here in front of my house. It's so shocking." She handed me a cup of coffee.

I could only agree.

Ruiz was still on the phone when the doorbell rang, and a few seconds later Wembley joined us in Stella's living room.

I set down my coffee and tried to surreptitiously exit the living room, hoping I could say my final goodbye and thank you to Stella in the hallway.

"Mallory, wait," Detective Ruiz said.

Nuts. I spun around. "Just heading home. You can find me there."

"You need to wait until an officer has taken your statement."

Wembley put his arm around my shoulders. "Can't you see she's upset?" I wilted a little under his arm, and Wembley said, "You can have an officer come by the house just as easily."

I gave the detective a wan smile—but he wasn't buying it. I un-wilted my posture and, with a firm tone, said, "Look, it's that or you can just talk to my attorney."

Ruiz hadn't asked me any questions—not yet. He'd been too busy talking to people on the phone about tracking the license plate number and our location and other details. And I wanted to avoid that conversation like no other.

"I'll send someone down shortly." But there was a suspicious glint in his eye.

I climbed into Wembley's bright blue VW Vanagon, shut the door, and groaned. "Save me."

Wembley started up the old van. "I think you've already managed that all on your own."

"Actually, it was surprisingly easy. I think I wasn't supposed to wake up so quickly." I let my head roll back against the headrest. "But that's not the most pressing issue. What am I supposed to tell the cops?"

"What happened?"

I thought about it. "Well, I don't know. A pulse of something knocked me out, but not before I grabbed hold of the detective." I shook my head. "And don't ask me why I did that."

"Ah. Well, first, you can simply say, 'I don't know,' because you don't. But I suspect you grabbed the detective to protect him." He tapped his forehead. "Precognition."

Wembley was determined to prove the existence of precognition as an enhancement. He'd halfway convinced me that I had some low-level precog skill. "Except how would I do that? I don't really have a way to protect myself from unknown magic." As I spoke, I realized I was a complete idiot. "My choker."

Wembley turned onto our street. "Yeah, and it probably would have kept you from short-circuiting if you hadn't spread the love."

"I actually am a little wigged by this whole thing, and my brains are a little scrambled. You're going to have to be a little clearer than that."

"That choker is intended to protect one person, and that one person is you. You extended the protection to another person, weakening its effectiveness."

"Oh." I had to think about that, because...no. "See, that can't be right, because I'd have to know that the choker protected anyone I was touching. And that the pulse thingy was an attack. I mean, maybe my spidey senses kicked in to warn me—I do have a vague memory of moving really fast right before it hit me—but no way I'd know about the choker. It's not like Star gave me an instruction booklet with the thing."

Wembley smiled. "Precognition."

I covered my face with my hands as Wembley pulled into our drive and then into the garage. When the van rolled to a stop, I uncovered my face and said, "That's crazy, Wembley."

He hopped out, looking way too pleased with himself. "It's proof."

"Hardly." I eyed the garage suspiciously as I got out of the van. The place still gave me the heebie-jeebies, since I knew Wembley stored his blood out here. I tiptoed past the huge fridge—and I felt cray-cray the entire time.

Once we were inside and I wasn't so stressed out by the presence of what I suspected was a massive blood store, I had a thought. A potentially revolutionary thought. "Why not tell the guy the truth? Kill several birds with one stone: he gets the truth about my progenitor and ends his obsessed hunt for the already dead serial killer, we get a potentially useful source inside the force who can help us find both Akira and Patrick-Elvis, and I don't have to lie my pants off."

Wembley grinned.

"What?"

"Freudian slip? Does someone have a little crush on the detective?" Wembley retrieved a bottle of spicy veggie juice from the fridge and chucked it at me.

I hadn't even realized I was hungry, but I downed it in a few gulps. "No crush, but he is attractive."

"Well, your plan is terrible. If you tell him the truth, there's no guarantee he'll believe you. And, if he does, that he's capable of handling the reality of our world."

"How much trouble would I be in if I did happen to let it slip?"

"It depends on how trustworthy he is, if you're willing to vouch for him, if he's willing to submit to a formal attestation by an experienced witch. There are a number of factors. But I'm telling you: don't do it."

"Oh, yeah, Bradley just did that attestation thing." I sidestepped the implied question.

Wembley gave me a warning look.

I threw my hands up in the air. "Fine. Not a peep from me." A knock interrupted us. "That didn't take long."

It had to be the cops, here for my statement, so I got up to answer the door. Wembley trailed along behind me. I had a feeling he was going to act like a mother hen for a little while, what with me being nabbed on our front lawn.

I checked the peephole first, and it most certainly wasn't the cops. I swung open the door. "Alex, what's up?"

He pushed the door open wider and walked in. "You getting kidnapped. Which I heard about from Wembley, not you."

"I just got home maybe five minutes ago? I haven't had time, and I'm not sure when Wembley did." I glanced down the hall, but the sneaky turkey had disappeared. "Come on in. You can hover and make me feel like an idiot."

He followed me into the kitchen, because I was hungry again and needed a little pick-me-up. "Mostly I'd like to know why your protection charm failed."

"Yeah, about that—Wembley explained that it might

have something to do with me grabbing the detective before I was zapped." I glanced at Alex before I grabbed a spicy veggie juice from the fridge. Yep, he did not look happy.

"That weakens the charm."

"I understand that now. But what if I hadn't? Then who knows what that magic tidal wave would have done to him? Besides, I'm pretty sure the choker still worked. I woke up almost right away. I mean, he didn't even tie us up or anything. I'm sure we were supposed to be out for a lot longer."

"He? Did you see him?"

Had I seen him? There'd been a pulse of magic, then I woke up in the bed of the truck. "No, I never saw him. Wait, I did see the truck, and then the truck was driving toward us..." I searched my mind for some image of the person behind the wheel. "No, I didn't see him, or I didn't notice him. But I'm sure it was a man who did this."

Alex helped himself to a glass and juice in the fridge. "You want to know what would have happened if you hadn't tried to protect the detective? Your protection charm likely would have protected you from the attack and you'd have been able to defend yourself."

"And Detective Ruiz?"

"Conveniently unconscious while you and Tangwystl kicked some kidnapper's butt." He took a sip of grape juice.

I gave him a squinty look. "You're guessing. You can't know the magic our baddie used wouldn't kill a mundane. You can't begin to imagine my guilt if the detective croaked while I was playing my-sword-is-bigger-than-yours."

But the argument didn't seem to sway him. If anything, he looked more pissed off. "You're not much help to anyone if you're dead."

The doorbell rang. I raised my eyebrows and said, "I thought I was harder to kill these days."

As I walked to the door, I heard him reply, "Harder, not impossible."

I opened the door without checking the peephole, because I was annoyed and flustered and it just didn't occur until the door was already open.

And there was Detective Ruiz.

"I thought you were sending someone to take my statement. Isn't it a conflict of interest for you to do it?" I put my hands on my hips. "You were a victim, in case you've forgotten."

The detective did not look amused. "Oh, I think you want to give *me* your statement. Especially the part about your glowing necklace, how you can move so fast you look like a blur of color, and maybe why I couldn't see the face of the driver, even though his truck was only a few feet away."

WHAT'S A VAMP WITHOUT THE BLOOD DRINKING?

O ops.

Detective Ruiz stood in the doorway and waited for me to respond to his list of impossible events. That he witnessed firsthand.

Big oops.

My hands fell from my hips. "I'm not sure what you're accusing me of."

He arched a dark eyebrow. "Who said I was accusing you of anything? Are you going to invite me in? I do need an *official* statement."

I narrowed my eyes and gave him my best you-can't-intimidate-me look. Except he could, he could definitely intimidate me. I'd been a vamp barely over a month now, and I was already involved in my second potential reveal scandal. I opened the door wider.

"Mr. Valois." Detective Ruiz nodded.

I spun around to find Alex only a few feet behind me, and then Wembley joined him. *They* couldn't be intimidated.

Hm. Perhaps this was bad. Perhaps de-escalation was in order. "Hang on, everyone. Let's just take a seat in the living room, why don't we?"

Wembley didn't look too terribly concerned, and he was the first to turn and move toward the living room.

Alex and the detective were a hair slower, and when they did, it was clear neither of them was comfortable with the other.

Wembley took the armchair, which left the couch and the second armchair. Alex commandeered the sofa, leaving the second armchair for the detective. I felt like we were all participating in some ritual that was clear to all the participants but me.

I sat down on the opposite end of the sofa from Alex. "So, all I can say is that I don't really remember what happened. I walked out to get something out of my car, we were talking, so I continued out to the curb, then I was waking up in the back of a pickup truck."

Detective Ruiz didn't pull out a notepad or a pen or a recording device. He just sat in the armchair, his forearms resting on his thighs and his hands clasped. "That's your story?"

"What do you expect? She's suffered through a traumatic event, and memory can be a tricky thing." The double meaning in Alex's reply wasn't lost on me. If the detective didn't drop this, Alex would have the guy's memory wiped.

Which was a mistake. Ruiz practically sounded like a believer, like he was already in on the paranormal, enhanced-living secret. I didn't think he was the kind of guy to have a mental breakdown if he got the big reveal, because he seemed to be looking for exactly those answers.

"Magic is real," I said.

Wembley groaned, and Alex blinked then sat there with a blank expression.

"You think? What I want to know is what it has to do with us being kidnapped today. And what it has to do with the death of eleven women."

I stared till my eyeballs itched. Then I realized I was sitting in the midst of a very loud silence. I cleared my throat. I couldn't believe the guys were going to let the newbie vamp tackle this. "So...how do you feel about vampires?"

"That depends on what exactly a vampire is." Ruiz's eyes were darting between the three of us.

"This isn't your first exposure to the weird and wonderful, is it, Detective Ruiz?" Wembley *finally* jumped in.

"It is not." Surprise, surprise. The obsessive, justice-loving detective had a history with the enhanced community.

"A vampire is a person who's been infected with a virus that results in significant physiological changes." I was rather proud of myself. That was worthy of Bradley.

"And consumes blood? I mean, what's a vampire without the blood-drinking?" A small smile played about the detective's lips.

He was definitely not about to have a mental breakdown. I shot Alex an I-told-you-so look, but he didn't budge. He looked just as cranky and put out as before.

"Yes, in a non-lethal way, of course." Wembley smiled politely.

"Well, mostly in a non-lethal way," I said. "That case you've been hounding me about—"

"Two interviews is hardly hounding."

"Arresting me when you know I didn't do it definitely qualifies as hounding. But more importantly, the man you're looking for—the one who killed all of those women—is dead. He was a vampire."

Wembley lifted a finger. "A rogue vampire, who has been punished for his crimes."

I bit my lip to keep from commenting on exactly which Society laws my progenitor had broken, because it definitely wasn't the one Ruiz would assume. Multiple murders? No big deal. Sloppy murder that left clues about the existence of vampires? That one triggered the Society's death penalty.

Alex had been silent—peevishly so. But he must have decided our little chat had gone on long enough, because he said, "Of course, we can't let you tell anyone." Except it didn't come out peevish. It was menacing. And he looked a little scary.

Detective Ruiz's eyes narrowed. "Is that a threat?"

"A guarantee," Alex said. "We protect our own, and that means secrecy. Besides"—he smiled with nothing resembling humor—"your silence is in both groups' best interests."

"Agreed."

All three of us stared at the detective with varying degrees of mistrust. That was much too easy.

"I get it," Ruiz said. "I deal with discrimination, prejudice, and violence all day long. I get it."

But Alex wasn't buying it. And Wembley hardly looked convinced.

I mean—did I believe him?

"Look," Ruiz said, "I had a partner. His wife...she was different." Not like you guys"—he pointed at me and Wembley—"more like you, Valois. And one day she was gone. Went to live with her mother, he said. Except she didn't. I checked. But this was a long time ago, and I didn't make a good choice. I walked away."

I felt a terrible sadness—well out of the proportion for the story, because I didn't know that woman, but it pulled at my heart. "You think the husband found out and killed her."

"I do. Especially given some things I've learned since, both about him and about the— What did you call it? The weird and wonderful?"

But the detective shouldn't be experiencing the weird and wonderful world of enhanced living on any kind of regular basis. He was human. A human who had lumped me and Wembley together...

"Holy cow. You can see magic, can't you?" I couldn't believe it. This mundane cop could pick up on what kind of magic enhanced people had, and I couldn't even begin to guess at how that was done. "Is he—"

"No," Wembley said. "Completely unenhanced human."

"I told you, I saw the necklace glow, the wave of purple light—"

"What?" Alex leaned forward. "What purple light?"

"The one that knocked us out."

Alex turned to me. "You didn't say anything about a purple light."

I threw my hands up. "How? How was I supposed to tell you about something I *didn't see*? And how is this guy able to see magic that I can't if he's so human?" I hitched my thumb in Ruiz's direction.

"Hey, watch it. This isn't my fault. You're the one who withheld vital information in an ongoing investigation." The detective turned to Alex. "What does the purple light mean?"

"Definitely human," Wembley murmured.

"The purple light means he was physically here and using a lot of magic, probably witch magic," Alex said.

"Yeah," Wembley said. "Witch magic does tend more toward lights and sparkles."

I bit my tongue yet again. Both Wembley and Alex had seen the blue-green lights and sparkles I'd created. Wembley when he'd given me Tangwystl, and Alex when we'd pinky sworn to not reveal each other's secret. And then there was my other witchlike ability to call Tangwystl, even though the sword had never been bound to me in a way that would make that possible. Also the freaky garlic tears. Although that one might actually be vampy, depending—

"Wait a second." My list of improbable and witchlike abilities brought a question to mind. "Can witches be men?"

Now I got the awkwardly silent stare. I frowned at Ruiz. He certainly shouldn't be all judgy. How would he know if witches could be men?

"Can vampires be women?" Ruiz asked. "Everyone who's a vampire, raise your hand."

I couldn't believe it, but Wembley stuck his hand in the air. Maybe he'd been sneaking coffee all morning long when I hadn't been looking.

Wembley grinned at me, so I snorted and raised my hand.

I put my hand back down. "But that's not fair. I happen to know one kind of enhanced being that can only be a woman. So there," my inner twelve-year-old added.

"Witches can be men," Alex said. "Or rather, men can become witches. But for every five female witches, there's maybe one male."

"Ha!" I pumped the air with my fist. "See? What did I tell you? Witches are *mostly* women." Alex's mouth had a funny, pinched look, so I quickly added in a more subdued tone, "So, ah, Detective Ruiz, what is it that you see that lets you know someone has magic?"

"It's a vapor that hangs around some people, thicker, thinner, different shades from white, black, and all sorts of colors. And I don't see it all the time. I only saw yours once, but I'd say it was more like Wembley's." Looking at Alex, he said, "Yours is pretty dark. And depressing."

Alex didn't comment, but Wembley nodded, as if none of this was a huge surprise to him. "Interesting. For some it's an odor, others it's colored lights. You never know."

I looked around the group and decided it was time to wager on a good outcome, which included preserving the obsessively righteous detective's memory. "So can we all agree that I was right, and Detective Ruiz should join the fold?"

Alex and Wembley replied simultaneously—too bad their answers were different.

"Thanks for not being an idiot, Wembley." I glared at Alex.

"You do understand that there's a serious conflict of interest at issue here," Ruiz said. "Regardless of how much I may believe it's in everyone's best interest to keep this secret, my first duty is to the law. And my name's Gabe."

Why be so brutally honest? I wanted to tell him to shush or they'd make his brain mush, but that didn't seem wise at this particular juncture. I gave him a second look and realized he was pretty tense. Maybe he did realize on some level that he was in a serious mess, and he was simply that honest.

I did not want to like this guy any more than I already did. He was a nuisance, at the very least, but more likely he was a danger to the community.

"We police our own," Alex said.

"Which might be fine—to the point where your community's laws and human law agree. But when they diverge?" Detective Ruiz—Gabe—looked earnest. And conflicted.

The guy had been carrying a doozy of a secret around for a while: magic existed and he could see it. And he'd been carrying around some pretty stout guilt. He also didn't seem to have a problem with bending the rules in pursuit of a greater good—witness my arrest and his off-the-record visit today. All of those things boded well for his future silence, but he needed to say the words.

"We can erase your memories," Alex said.

Gabe clasped his hands together. "That resolves nothing. Your people are still flying below the legal radar, and I can still see magic."

I could feel my face scrunching up in sympathy. "Except they don't need your permission to remove those memories, not when the safety of the Society is in question."

Gabe didn't respond. He didn't have to. We both knew it was a terrible thing, and, regardless, the Society would do what was necessary for the protection of its members.

"Join us or forget us. Those are the options." Alex didn't comment on whether he'd be supporting Gabe's continued interaction with the Society.

"Humph." It whooshed past my lips before I could edit myself.

"Yes, Mallory?" Alex's tone was sharp. He wasn't happy about any part of this situation.

"Well," I said, "there's no point to him pitching in with us if you're not willing to make a supporting recommendation. I don't see Cornelius buying any endorsement I make, and besides, I think I've stretched my credibility as far as possible with Bradley."

"She's not wrong. And my support would likely be detrimental." Wembley kicked back in his chair, propping his ankle on his knee. "It would be interesting to have someone with an eye for magic inside the police. The last guy aged out and had to be moved about five years ago."

Gabe eyed Wembley. "You had a magical source on the force?" When Wembley nodded, Gabe asked, "And aging out, what is that?"

"Most of us don't age, or age more slowly, with some exceptions. So we can't stay in one place for too long, not without assuming a new identity and sometimes having surgery done."

Gabe nodded as if that made complete sense to him. He didn't seem to have the same hang-ups with magical plastic surgery that I'd had. "I need some time to consider everything. Besides, we're in the middle of a case—one that might be best solved with my memory intact."

"Give me just a minute," Alex said as he stood up and pulled out his phone. He disappeared into the kitchen, probably to call Cornelius.

I'd know for sure if I had vamp super-hearing. But my non-blood-drinking, not-a-predator self didn't have that nifty skill.

I almost asked Gabe about my choker glowing and the purple light, but then I figured Alex would want to hear whatever else he had to say, if anything. So Wembley hung out in his chair eyeballing Gabe curiously, but otherwise looking relaxed, and I tried not to drown in the awkward silence.

At least Gabe wasn't all tense and spooked. I would have been in his place—except I hadn't lived my life knowing freaky stuff that had no rational explanation was all around me.

He caught my gaze and said, "It's good to have proof finally. I mean—I knew, but..."

Alex came back before I could respond, but the look on Gabe's face tugged at my heart. We couldn't take away these memories, not when he finally had proof of something he'd suspected existed for so long.

Alex handed me a small bottle of organic carrot juice. "Don't give me the sad puppy-dog eyes." Shifting his attention to Gabe, Alex said, "Cornelius has agreed to give you a week if you'll come in to formalize the agreement. With any luck, we'll have our case wrapped up by then and you can either go your own way—or you can become a source."

Gabe's nostrils flared, but he recovered his poker face almost immediately. "When you say your case, you mean the kidnapping? You think you can find the kidnapper in less than a week?"

"We've got an open case with two missing people," Alex said. "If the kidnap attempt is connected—and I think it is—Mallory was the likely target. Unless you know a reason you'd be the target of a magical attack?"

Gabe shook his head. "I've never said a word about what I can see. Not to anyone." A look of confusion crossed his face. "Why take me?"

"That's a good question," Wembley said. "I'd think you were an unplanned-for inconvenience, and I'd bet you weren't intended to survive the attack."

Alex's gaze met mine. "If a human shouldn't have survived the wave of magic, and then the detective goes on to live—"

"Ugh. That might explain why he bothered to take both of us. Gabe might have confused him by both looking human and surviving. And then there's me with the blood aversion. Yeah." I squeezed my eyes shut. "We'd fit the bill for unique enhanced people."

"Except I'm not enhanced," Gabe said. Then he nailed

me with a searching look. "Wait, you have a blood aversion?"

"Yep, but it's not something I advertise."

Wembley snorted. "You can hardly hide it. The greenish skin and puking are a dead giveaway."

I shrugged. He wasn't wrong.

"You've got a guy collecting unique magical beings—for something like a zoo?" Gabe seemed equal parts fascinated and appalled by the concept.

It was one possible explanation, except that would make me the zoo animal. No thanks. "Watch it, buddy. I'm not a panda bear to be ogled and fed bamboo shoots."

Gabe didn't seem to know what to say to that, and surprisingly, it was Alex who came to his rescue. "No one's calling you a panda. I know you have a particular aversion to being compared to furry mammals, but try to focus."

I'd show him focus. Turning to Gabe, I said in my sweetest voice, "Maybe you can help us find out if there have been any other victims. Alex hasn't been able to."

"Give me a break," Alex said. "I haven't had time to search, what with you abusing your protection charm and almost getting kidnapped."

"Children," Wembley said, "give it a rest. Let's hear what the detective can do to move the case forward, why don't we?"

"I can definitely look for potential victims. Help firm up the pattern, maybe provide some additional insight into the perpetrator through the connections between the victims. I'll start by pulling missing persons profiles. What time frame are we looking at?"

Alex motioned for Gabe to follow him. "The two cases we have are both within the last three days. We need to head over to Society headquarters to formalize the temporary agreement. You can go now?"

"Yeah. Although, Mallory, you do need to go down to the station and give a statement." Without even a hint of shame, he said, "No way I can take your statement; it's definitely a conflict of interest."

"I knew it." I debated for just a millisecond about not warning him, but I couldn't do it. Even though he had acted like a shifty turkey butt. "Hey, just a heads-up. Cornelius, the guy you're going to see, he's going to bind you in some magical way to ensure you keep your promise. No clue what the consequences for breaking the bind are, but I *do* know it would be a bad idea. So just be sure you're ready to keep quiet before you agree to anything."

I gave Alex a squinty look, and he held his hands up. "I'd have told him. Swear."

Gabe smiled at me and said, "Thanks." His gorgeous smile didn't quite make up for playing me, but it was a nudge in the right direction. Shifty or no, I wanted to like the guy.

Now if Cornelius would just not break him or freak him out with his creepy mercury eyes and Gabe could manage to stay alive until he got the knack of hanging out with a bunch of enhanced beings, he might turn out to be a great addition to the sleuthing team.

17

CHARMING HISTORY

Alex and Gabe had only been gone a few minutes when I decided that one small bottle of carrot juice wasn't gonna cut it. As I went to the kitchen, Wembley followed, and Boone—who'd probably been crashed out on my bed—ambled along behind.

"What is this? A babysitting conspiracy?"

Boone had the audacity to wag his tail, confirming my suspicion.

"How are you in on this? You didn't even hear about the zap and grab earlier." I looked into his deep brown eyes buried in his smooshy-skinned face, but couldn't get a read.

"I bet he can feel the stress vibes you're projecting." Wembley retrieved two glasses and the bottle of Macallan we hadn't quite finished off a few days ago. "You should get out more—not today, but generally. Meet some more people."

I eyed the bottle warily. We needed to find Akira and Patrick-Elvis. Granted, I couldn't do much, since I was now officially a target—but drinking just seemed wrong. Then I realized what Wembley was saying. "Wait a second. I have options."

"What do you mean?"

"Dating. I have dating options. That is what we're talking about it, isn't it? Isn't 'meeting' code for dating?"

Wembley just shrugged with one shoulder.

I glared back. "I meet men."

I could think of two hot men off the top of my head. Gabe, for one. Sure, he was a lying turkey butt, but generally speaking, I think he wanted to do the right thing—catch the bad guy, find justice for victims of crime, keep the populace safe, and all that white-hat stuff—he just had an ends-means problem.

And then there was my sword instructor. Muscles to die for, with some sword-wielding awesomeness thrown in for fun. Yum. And he didn't wear a wedding ring.

Two attractive, available—so far as I knew—and decent guys.

"And what does Alex think about them?"

"Who, what?" I focused back on Wembley and not on the mental image of bulging biceps.

"You meeting men. You having options. I was just wondering what Alex thought about these men. Is your blood sugar getting low? I've got a few of those vegan shakes you like in the fridge."

I was not admitting to fantasizing about bulging muscles, so I pressed my lips together and headed for the fridge. "Wonder how they go with Macallan."

When I turned around from the fridge with not one, but two vegan shakes, I saw the look of horror on Wembley's face.

"Just kidding. I'll finish these first. And why are you asking about Alex? He doesn't have any interest in me, not that kind of interest. He's more a..." Was there a nice way to say *screw 'em and leave 'em kind of guy*?

Wembley nodded. "He is about chasing the next shag. But you're wrong that he wouldn't care."

I waved a hand at him dismissively. "He's had plenty of opportunity to express shagging interest in me, and he hasn't." I squinted at Wembley. "Have you been watching Austin Powers again?"

Wembley gave me an innocent look. Clearly, he'd ignored my strong recommendation to hold off on the Austin Powers marathons. "Austin Powers isn't the point. I'm saying you may be of more than passing, shaggable interest to Alex. First, you're friends. Not like he has many. Second, you can't have missed how much you've influenced him."

"Sorry, how have *I* influenced Alex?" I was the guppy to Alex's shark, so I was pretty sure Wembley had been imbibing more than his share of coffee today.

Wembley's bushy brows rose in unabashed surprise. "You're kidding, right?"

Since I hadn't a clue what he was talking about, clearly I was not. I cocked my head and waited for the reasoning behind his bizarre assertion.

Wembley sighed. "He's pleasant when you're around— amiable, almost likable. And he's happier. I heard him *laugh* the other day. Everyone's noticed the change."

I blinked in astonishment. "How am I supposed to know he's not like that when I'm not around? I'm *not around*. And, sorry, but I don't think so."

"You make him happy."

That was silly. Sure, we had a certain connection that he didn't have with most people. I knew his secret, for one. Being spirit haunted because you'd made a few bad wizardly choices as a kid sucked the big one. Especially when childhood was so brief, and the lifespan of a wizard wasn't.

"I mean, we're close...sort of. But I can't imagine he's all *that* different with me."

Wembley raised an eyebrow. "Unpleasant. Cranky, snappish, short-tempered—"

"I got it."

"Basically all the time. The man lives in one long, never-ending bad mood."

"I said, I got it." But I didn't. I found it hard to believe I was such a strong influence on a guy I considered pretty self-contained. And we weren't even intimate...not physically. But I'd talked the guy down from exorcising a demon that had possessed him—and as a small, barely noticeable side effect, *killing himself*—so I guessed I was close with the guy.

"Have you talked yourself out of your denial yet?"

I looked up, surprised to see that Wembley had poured us both a scotch. "Maybe. It's just a strange thought. He's so..."

"A man unto himself. Yeah, I do know the guy."

I sipped my scotch and considered his comments. As the warmth of the liquid hit my tongue, I considered that he might be right; maybe Alex was happier around me.

Maybe I judged less. Maybe he could tell how much I liked and respected him—because as annoying as the guy could be, I did. Or maybe it was as simple as our shared secrets. I hoped Wembley was right, because I truly believed Alex deserved his own slice of happiness, however he came by it.

I tapped the table with my index finger. "Hey, if I'm stuck here for now, we need to at least review our suspect list and consider our clues. That's the ninja-sleuthing thing to do."

"Fair enough. Go."

"First, we've got our victim list. For sure Akira, likely Patrick-Elvis, Detective Ruiz and my failed kidnapping, and the detective is going to hopefully hook us up with a list based on missing persons files. Next, suspects. Ralph is a weak contender, but Anton is working on that one. Patrick-Elvis is certainly connected, but I'm convinced he's a victim." I wrinkled my nose. "I really liked him."

"Persuasion. It's a demigod power."

"Makes sense." But I still hated that my emotional response to someone might have been so blatantly manipulated.

"You know, Ralph has no power. How does our guy subdue, maybe kill, a demigod and a kitsune?" Wembley sipped at his scotch then swirled it in his mouth. "I'd think it would be difficult to knock one out. But if our kidnapper can incapacitate Elvis and a nine-tailed kitsune, then—"

"He's likely not Ralph. Wait, what does nine-tailed mean? That's the second time I've heard it."

"In the kitsune world, nine-tailed is powerful."

I was so not powerful—and a target. My hand reached for my choker.

"Yeah, being prepared with protection charms can certainly help. Especially one of Star's; she's good." Wembley downed a solid slug of scotch. "That's a gorgeous piece, worn by an equally gorgeous woman many years ago."

"It has a history?"

Wembley smiled. "Of course. The best protection charms do, and they're imbued with a hint of the former owner's personality. That one is an interesting choice for you. The woman who owned it—the original owner— wasn't a vamp. She was a wizard."

"Really?" I stared at him in amazement. "How is it even possible that you know that? It's a piece of jewelry. It could have come from anywhere in the world. Been owned by anyone."

"It certainly wasn't owned by just anyone; it belonged to Louisa, a beautiful woman with an even lovelier soul."

"Sounds like someone had a crush." I peeked over my glass's rim as I sipped my scotch.

"Sure, I was a little in love. Everyone was. But then she died." His voice flattened out.

I ran my thumb along the velvet band, and for once my curiosity didn't get the best of me. I didn't want to know what terrible thing had brought about her death. And it had been something awful; I could see it on Wembley's face.

"She possessed a warmth that I see in you, too." He closed his eyes, and when he opened them, it was like that past—with whatever horror it held—hadn't been. "It's a great choice for you."

My hand fell away from the soft choker. "I picked it. Star wasn't keen to make a choice for me, so she had me sort through her bins of charms."

"Really? Now that's fascinating." Wembley grinned. "That's not how it's usually done. And I can only imagine how much an Edwardian piece like that would cost."

Oh, no. Those rhinestones... "They're real, aren't they?"

"The diamonds? I'm sure they are. You didn't know?"

"Oh, no. Not a clue. Alex is the one picking up the tab, so please tell me he's not broke."

Wembley laughed. "No. Definitely not broke. Anyone who's been around for more than a few decades figures out how to finance a lengthy existence...or they don't have one."

I touched the choker nervously. Did I even want to know how much the thing was worth? That was a lot of shiny bling, if it was real. "Oh, wow. I'm supposed to shower and bathe with this thing on."

"I'm sure Star has permeated the material with a preservation spell." Wembley swallowed the rest of his scotch and placed the glass with great deliberation on the table. "Besides, the piece loses its value and can't be used as a charm any longer if it's ruined or destroyed. All it takes is one quick slice of a blade and that velvet would be covered in blood...if it didn't have a preservation spell."

"Thanks for that, Wembley. I needed a reminder some psycho is after me." I pushed my half-consumed glass of scotch away and rested my forehead on the cool wood of the breakfast table. I was fine. The guy had failed, so I was perfectly safe. Right.

"It's not so bad as all that."

Easy for the berserker Viking guy with ninja sword skills to say. I sat up and called out, "Tangwystl!"

And there she was, on the table in front of me. Seeing her made me a little more comfortable.

Bad lady. Good sword.

"Why am I a bad lady?" I sat up straighter. "I'm not a bad lady."

"Uh, perhaps not, but is there any reason you've called your sword to the kitchen? Planning to chop up some carrots for the juicer, maybe?"

Humph. No cooking. Stabby stab.

I bit back a grin. "That's right, honey, no cooking. I wouldn't dare."

Liar, liar, hot pants. Dig up dead guy.

"Oh, yeah, well, I didn't dig up that dead guy with you, because we had shovels." I *would* have, but no point in dwelling on that. "It's not like we have to worry about dulling your blade, so really it comes down to pride, doesn't it, sweetie?"

No digging, no cooking. Stabby stab. Tangwystl blew a raspberry at me.

"Hey. You need to stop with the raspberries. Aren't you a little old for that? And besides, there's no one for you to stab right now. Wembley's the only one here."

Tangwystl let out a besotted sigh. Apparently Wembley was forgiven his carrot comment, because she was gaga over his mad Viking sword skills. The crush she had on Wembley —or his sword arm—was just weird.

"I believe your sword is dismayed by the lack of attention she's been receiving lately."

Tangwystl tittered.

"Good grief. Will you stop already?" I tapped Tangwystl's hilt with the tip of my index finger.

"What?" Wembley asked as he poured another drink. "I'm just sitting over here enjoying my scotch."

"Not you. You know, she's more upset about her inability to spill blood regularly than the inattention. Never mind." I placed my hand on Tangwystl's hilt and gave her an affectionate rub. She drove me a little nuts, but she was a peach to have around when I was in a pinch.

"Let's hope that your detective's missing persons list proves informative."

I frowned. "He's not mine. I guess he did arrest me. And then he did get attacked and kidnapped with me...and escaped with me." I could see the trend. But that didn't make him mine.

"Sure, if you say so. Either way, I'll be interested to see what he comes up with."

I ticked the few clues we had off on my fingers. "Well, until then, we've got: a pattern of victims that includes three uniquely magical Society members, a cryptic message from Akira—"

"Wait, have you considered that you don't have three uniquely magical Society members as targets? What if you weren't the target? The detective is far from common: a mundane who can see magic."

"He wouldn't have been in the app either, I'm sure." I thought about it for a second and realized I didn't know who exactly had seen the contents of the app. Supposedly Cornelius had it destroyed, but wouldn't he have reviewed the information first? Or made some kind of copy?

I pulled out my phone and texted Bradley. He responded immediately.

"Uh-oh. You won't believe this. Detective Ruiz was in the app, probably. Sort of." I shook my head and read Bradley's text out loud. "'Jose Gabriel Ruiz is listed as having the sight.'"

"That could be Gabe's dad or his uncle. Are you calling Alex or am I?" Wembley asked.

Since the Society's headquarters was just minutes away, the two men had certainly already arrived. Better to give him a heads-up, just in case Cornelius turned squirrelly and wasn't sharing information.

Alex picked up on the first ring. "Hey, how'd you find out so quickly?"

"About Detective Ruiz? Wait, what are you talking about?"

"No," Alex said. "About the coma patient. What were you calling about?"

"To tell you that there's a Ruiz in Bradley's app. You know, just in case Cornelius didn't mention it."

"Ah, no, that's new information, and hopefully means you're not a target."

I clenched my teeth. No acknowledgment that the probable target was stuck to his side for the next little while. "Tell me about this coma patient. What do they have to do with our case?" I tapped speaker and set my phone down.

"The patient's been identified as Sofia Kontos. She was enhanced, a phoenix. Anton is on his way to check on her."

"What do you mean, she was enhanced?"

Wembley leaned in closer. "Wembley here. I'll explain it to her. You get the detective squared somewhere safe, and I'll load up Mallory, Tangwystl, and Boone and head over to headquarters."

When I looked down at my phone, I realized Alex had hung up.

"What the heck is going on?"

"A phoenix is a creature of fire. You can't wound the physical embodiment of a phoenix—kill the physical body, yes, but any non-mortal injury is healed. Think regenerated through fire. So if Sofia's physical body is in a coma, something is terribly wrong with her magic. Most likely, it's diminished or depleted."

"Are you saying our kidnapper is a magic-sucking parasite?"

"I hadn't thought about it that way—but that's certainly one explanation."

18

WHEN CAFFEINE IS NOT A VAMP'S FRIEND

I'm a vampire—even if a weirdly non-parasitic one—so was it odd I leaped to a vampiric conclusion right away? It was right there at the top of my brain, so not odd at all. Wembley, on the other hand, had different ideas. Coincidence that he was also the human-life-juice-sucking one of the two of us? I thought not. Maybe someone wasn't as comfortable with their biological imperatives as they liked to think.

En route to the Society's headquarters, Wembley came up with a half-dozen other explanations for Sofia's damaged or missing magic, none of which involved sucking the magic-juice essence from an enhanced being. A plague that attacked magic, an assertion of will by Sofia to remain in the injured state (why would *anyone* do that?), a sleeping sickness that Sofia's phoenix didn't perceive as illness or injury, just to name a few.

I put my turn signal on and slowed down. "I think you're grasping. The guy we want is a collector. Why collect people to infect them?"

"Worse things have been done in history for the advancement of science, to satisfy curiosity, and for no logical reason at all."

"I don't know. I'm just thinking, if I were an evil collector of uniquely gifted magical beings, what would be my motivation? Can't show them off to my evil buddies, because the chances are slim I even have buddies. I could store them to gaze upon with sick adoration, but then why the coma? Why not just kill them?" I turned into the parking lot of the Society's headquarters.

"That's actually a thought. Maybe the coma is a byproduct of how he's storing his victims."

I parked in the Bits, Baubles, and Toadstools part of the parking lot. It was the easiest—and most entertaining—way to get into headquarters. "How does someone induce coma in a demigod, a kitsune, and a phoenix?"

"I'm not sure."

I hesitated before getting out of the Jeep. "You're not sure, there are so many choices? Or you're not sure, you haven't a clue?"

"I'm not sure of one method, because I'd use a different one for each of them. Surround the phoenix in an ice bath, cool her core body temperature down low enough and fast enough, and you might be able to neutralize her. Might. And that's not even considering the logistics of such a task."

I turned to look at him. "You are a devious dude, Wembley."

"Lots of experience." Though he didn't deny being devious.

I got out and walked around to the back. Before I let Boone out, I grabbed Tangwystl, all tucked up in her sheath, and slung her around my back. "Okay, buddy, your turn."

Boone waited patiently for me to clip the leash to his

collar. He seemed pleased to be out the house, even though he wasn't working.

"I need to get Boone out more."

"Neglecting your hound and your sword." Wembley made a tsking sound.

"Don't even start, old man."

I stopped in front of the Bits, Baubles, and Toadstools front door and turned to Boone. "If you need to—"

He didn't even wait for me to ask. He shook his whole body, from head to tail, one big, wiggling shake. Hair, dander, and slobber flew every which way. When the funk had settled, he headed to the front door.

Wembley swung it wide. "Maybe it's time for a bath?"

"Hey, he's clean." I hoped he was, because he'd been hanging out on my bed a lot. Hm. "But yeah, maybe we'll squeeze that in as soon as we're not in the midst of an imminent catastrophe." I looked around for Mandy, but couldn't find her.

We headed through the Employees Only door and down the hall to Alex's office.

"You know, I didn't see Alex's Juke in the parking lot. I wonder if he's taken the detective someplace else." Although where? Headquarters seemed the safest place to be. I knocked on his office door then opened it and poked my head in. "Alex? Gabe?"

Wembley pushed the door open further from behind me. "If he didn't want us to go in, he wouldn't have left it unlocked."

Michelle and Francis must have found a better place to hang out, because she wasn't anywhere to be seen. Boone strolled in like he owned the place and hopped up on Alex's futon. Then he curled up in a red, furry ball.

"I'm not sure that's a good idea. You know what? Never mind. Make yourself at home."

Wembley started opening Alex's desk drawers. "Doesn't he have some emergency booze in here? I thought there was—" He smiled and held aloft a bottle of some kind of liquor.

"No thanks," I said when he tipped the bottle in my direction. "You do realize we're in the middle of a case, right?"

A muffled thud sounded in the distance.

"No, you're in the middle of a case. I'm babysitting you until Alex gets back." He moved over to the kitchen and started to hunt for a glass in the cabinets. "Aha, and here's a note, conveniently left in his kitchen nook—because why would he text?"

I shrugged. "He probably thought he'd be back before us."

"Well, he's gone to drop the detective off at the station. Seems Gabe wouldn't agree to hide out at here, so he got an escort to the one place they both figured he'd be safe for a few hours."

"Makes sense, I gue—"

The door to Alex's office flew open.

I saw the black T-shirt first. Def Leppard. And no face, but a gun. The gun was all I could see.

I pulled Tangwystl from her sheath—too late. He'd fired. I felt nothing, no pain, no awareness of being hit.

I glanced down, looking for the blood that had to be there. But there was nothing. I'd felt no pain, because I hadn't been shot. *Wembley* had. He staggered, then steadied himself. And I tried to remember that everything would be fine, because Wembley was a vamp.

I didn't have time to consider whether Wembley was

bulletproof, because a snarling, raging blur of red flew past me. Boone's baying barks reverberated off the walls.

This was bad. Really bad. Teeth versus gun was a very bad outcome for my dog. Quicker than a blink, I advanced —but that moment of hesitation had been too much, and canine screams of pain filled the room.

Flame-covered hands twisted and pulled at my dog.

I saw red. *Burn my dog? I'll rip your head off.* "Tangwystl, give me an edge. A very sharp edge."

Off with his head!

But before I got that far, the faceless slime had the nerve to shoot me. At least I'd distracted him from Boone, who'd limped away and collapsed in a corner.

Being shot didn't feel at all like I thought it would. A punch, plus a sting, and a rushing warmth zipping through my body. Adrenaline? I looked down to find a dart in my shoulder.

I yanked it out, and then I was there, right in his face, sword drawn.

He pulled a sword—from where, I don't know—and deflected my attack. I tried to remember what I'd learned from my instructor, but that just confused my mind, so I stopped.

Until he advanced, cutting across my torso. I lifted Tangwystl to deflect the blow, and thank goodness for muscle memory.

Soon my body found the familiar flowing rhythm, our blades meeting and the beats becoming not unlike a practice session...and neither of us made contact with flesh. Something was wrong—besides the fact that I kept hearing the song "Eye of the Tiger" in the background. He should be faster, probably better than me—shouldn't he? Everyone was better with a sword than me.

But as the thought entered my head, he disappeared. With preternatural speed, he'd fled to the door and then down the hallway. And "Eye of the Tiger" faded away.

If he could move that fast, shouldn't he have been able to take my head off?

I didn't even consider chasing him, because of Boone and Wembley. I sheathed Tangwystl, locked Alex's door, and then looked for something to barricade it—but the desk was too big and too far. What I'd give for a burst of normal vamp strength right about now. Wembley!

But Wembley was in no state to help me. He was standing in the same place—hadn't, in fact, moved throughout the swordplay, the music, or the bad-guy escape. And he was staring at his outstretched hand like it was the greatest wonder in the world.

"Wembley? Are you okay?"

But he didn't seem to hear me. I glanced over at Boone, and he didn't look so good. Heavy panting and a glazed look in his eyes meant he was either in shock, or so much pain he wasn't able to function. I squinted at him. He was panting red clouds of smoke. That couldn't be normal.

I pulled out my phone and called Alex. As the phone rang, I approached Wembley cautiously. He didn't seem to be concerned about me or even notice me. He'd stopped obsessing over his hands and seemed to be peering up at the light fixture now. Was that my Great-Aunt Lulu's reflection in the glass of the fixture?

"Hey, I'm just around the corner." Alex's voice snapped me back to reality. Was that a whiff of gingerbread cookies?

"Hurry. Boone's hurt, and Wembley's acting weird." I plucked out the dart from his chest and tossed it near Alex's desk. "Whoa. Wait a second—"

I dropped my phone and scrambled away from Wembley. As soon as I'd pulled out the dart, his fangs had descended, and he was staring at me with glowing red eyes.

"Wembley, it's me. It's Mallory? Your buddy, your roommate."

"What happened? Are you all right?" My phone was a few feet away, so Alex must have been screaming for me to hear him. And again with the gingerbread.

I raised the volume of my voice but tried to keep the tone calm. "Not really okay. Wembley's eyes are all red. I think he thinks I'm dinner." I didn't take my eyes off Wembley, and I was pretty sure he perked up at the mention of dinner. "Not food, Wembley. I have icky blood."

Oh no. That was when I remembered: vamps couldn't feed off vamps. Turned out that as nasty and parasitic as vamps were, they weren't cannibals.

"Any clue what my blood would do to him, Alex?"

"Nothing good, but probably worse for you. Almost there." I'd swear that every time I heard Alex's voice, the room got more gingerbready.

Gingerbread wasn't quite so pressing as a red-eyed Wembley, who'd almost come within sword reach. I pulled out Tangwystl. "I need a dull blade, Tangwystl. Very dull."

Pfft.

Wembley was walking toward me with deliberation. Yeah, I was being stalked.

"Seriously. Right now."

Off with his—

"Not now. This is Wembley we're talking about, sweetie."

No-no. Squishy like butter.

"Good girl." Not for the first time, I remembered Alex's critical comments about living swords: a sword is a tool, an implement that serves at the will of its master; free will changes the dynamic.

When Wembley got within striking range, I hit him with the flat of the blade, and it bounced off him like rubber. "Tangwystl! Dull, not child-safe."

Alex hadn't been wrong.

Unfortunately, that thwack with my rubberized sword had pissed off Wembley, and he was looking both hungry *and* angry now. At least he wasn't using his vamp super-speed. I kept Tangwystl raised between the two of us and began a slow retreat. For every step forward he took, I took one back. That worked out great until I backed myself into a wall.

Great-Aunt Lulu floated above Wembley's right shoulder and said, "This is going to hurt."

A split second later, Wembley ducked and grabbed my sword arm—and bit me.

My screech of pain about pierced my own ears. I couldn't imagine what it had sounded like to Alex, who—it turned out—was in the hallway. My screech was cut off by the small explosion that blew open the office door, revealing him on the other side.

For a second I forgot the pain, and I watched the office door smack the ground and skitter across the floor. Alex stood backlit in the door, and I had a feminine, girly epiphany: I was the damsel being rescued, and Alex was my hero.

Apparently that didn't sit well, because I had a knee-jerk response...literally. I kneed Wembley so hard in the junk that he stopped munching on my arm.

And when he let loose, the blood flowed and the pain came back in rush. I held my arm close to my body and sank to the floor. Only the wall was holding me up. Even so, I couldn't help a smirk at the sight off Wembley doubled over, clutching his manhood. "Serves you right."

Alex maneuvered himself in between me and Wembley. "If there was a rulebook, it would definitely include not taunting the crazed vamp."

"Yum. You smell like gingerbread."

"Are you high?"

"Oh!" Seeing Great-Aunt Lulu, hearing music that couldn't be there, and smelling scents that weren't either… "Yes, I think I am." My eyes narrowed. "That guy used a tranq gun to dose us both with caffeine."

When I looked up, I saw that Alex had Wembley in a bear hug. For now. It didn't look like it was going well for Alex. Which raised the question: who won when you pitted a drugged ex-berserker Viking vamp against a centuries-old sword-wielding wizard who wasn't using his sword? I groaned and started to look for my phone. It was halfway across the room. So far away.

I started the long crawl, and had made it a few feet when Great-Aunt Lulu said, "A little to the right, dear."

Who was I to argue with Great-Aunt Lulu? So I angled my crawl to the right. Two seconds later, I got a stout kick to my gut for my efforts—but Wembley was also on the ground. *Look at me, tripping the bad guy.* Well, the temporary bad guy.

"Sorry, Wembley," I mumbled, "but not really." My arm was burning like blazes. And I continued my crawl toward hopeful backup. By the time I made it to the phone, Wembley was back up and Alex had a few more bruises. I dialed Cornelius.

"Yes, Ms. Andrews. How can I assist you?"

"Help in Alex's office right now. Wembley's drugged, and he and Alex are fighting, and poor Boone isn't doing so good." I could still see the hazy red from the dog's panting.

"Slow down. Are you telling me that Alex and Wembley are engaged in combat in Alex's office?"

"Yes."

"I'm out of the office, but I'm sending Anton now. He's on the other side of the warehouse, but it should only be a few minutes. Tell me, calmly, what's happened?"

I took a breath with every intent of explaining it to him —truly, I meant to—but all that came out were sobs. My arm *hurt*. And my dog might not be okay. And my friends were fighting. I started the slow crawl—made slower by my hiccuping gasps of breath in between bouts of crying—to Boone's side.

I'd just planted myself next to Boone and gotten a solid tail wag in response, when I felt a zipping electricity in the air.

I turned to find Wembley several inches off the ground. He suddenly fell in a heap. The air shimmered around him and the room pulsed. I must have blinked, because the next thing I knew, Wembley was surrounded by incandescent bars. The glow faded, and what remained was almost translucent.

"Oh. My. God. You just made a cage out of air. That's not possible."

"Definitely possible." Alex pulled his cell from his pocket then dropped down on the futon. "Cornelius? We need someone in my office who can handle an angry, drugged vamp. Wembley." And then he hung up. "I guess you already called. Anton's on the way."

"Right. But you made a cage out of air." Sure, I was still over-caffeinated, but I didn't think that had anything to do with my inability to comprehend what had just happened.

Wembley grabbed the bars and shook them.

"A really strong, vamp-proof cage," I said.

"Yes." Alex nodded and leaned back against the cushions of the futon. "And you're wearing your protection charm, so how did this happen?"

"I got plugged with a dart—which didn't affect me like Wembley, because I'm caffeine tolerant—and then I got my arm chomped. All non-magical."

"You're semi-tolerant to caffeine. But speaking of your arm, you're dripping blood all over my floor. How about you grab the medical kit from my bathroom, and I'll take a look at it."

Shockingly, I didn't get all woozy and lightheaded over the sight of my blood. Granted, I wasn't looking too closely. I petted Boone carefully on one of his ears and then started to lean against the wall, using it as leverage to get myself into a standing position.

Once I'd made it into a fully upright position, I realized how incredibly unlike Alex it was to send me off wounded for supplies.

Asking me to fetch the med kit, lounging on his futon when Wembley was frothing at the mouth only a few feet away...

I took a closer look at him. "Uh, you don't look so good."

"Neither do you." I gave him the evil eye until he said, "Yeah, you wouldn't either if you'd just busted the laws of physics."

"Ah. So the air cage isn't one of your parlor tricks that you pull out to entertain the nieces and nephews around the holidays." I was trying to make light, but he was looking worse every second. His complexion was getting paler, and dark circles were blooming under his eyes. He almost looked like someone had punched him—in both eyes.

"Hardly a parlor trick. And I don't have nieces and nephews."

I skipped the supplies and made my way over to the futon instead. After I lowered myself down next to him, I said, "So, how bad is the bite?"

He took his T-shirt off and wrapped it around my arm. "Better if you don't bleed to death."

I snorted. "Pretty sure that can't happen. Wait—can it?"

He laughed, and it turned into a cough. "No. Not from this. But who knows how long it takes for you to manufacture blood? Probably longer than a blood-drinking vamp."

"Yeah, probably." I glanced at his tattooed chest. "You know Anton's on the way. And Wembley's out of his mind, but he might remember this."

Alex tipped his head in Wembley's direction. Wembley was huddled up, arms tucked around his knees, and his head rested against the solidified air bars. And he was snoring.

"Right. Well, Anton, anyway."

Alex shrugged. "Don't care. It's not such a secret, since one of my enemies has used it against me already. I shouldn't feel like I have to hide this from the people closest to me."

A deep throb that had started in my arm was spreading to the entirety of the right side of my body, and it was getting harder and harder to concentrate. "Before I do something stupid, like pass out, are you going to be okay?"

"You mean, am I going to be possessed?" He sighed. "I don't know. I don't think so. I'm tired, but—"

"You're not tired; you're exhausted." I could hardly miss that he couldn't sit up straight.

"Your concern is noted. My point is that while I'm tired"—he caught my gaze—"*very* tired, I'm not drunk. And therein lies the difference, as related to demon-possession.

Drunk, I have no defenses. Tired, I have weakened defenses."

"Yeah, if you're trying to reassure me, that's not really happening." I placed the back of my hand against his cheek. His skin was cool and dry to the touch, but the greyish tinge to his complexion wasn't helping his case.

"On the off chance I become susceptible at some point in the future, it would be handy to know that demon-wrangling trick of yours you used in our last case."

I moved over a few inches and rested my head on his shoulder. "If I ever figure it out, you'll be the first to know."

19

PHYSICS? WHAT PSYCHICS?

Another five or ten minutes passed before Anton showed up. But at least when he finally did, it turned out he'd had the sense to bring Francis, another enforcer, with him. Bonus, because I actually liked Francis, unlike Anton.

Neither one of them said a word about Alex's tattoos or even betrayed with a flickering glance that they thought them odd.

I tried to give Francis a reassuring smile. I must have missed the mark, because he grimaced in return. "Not looking your normal cheery self, are you?"

"Ow." Not what I'd planned to say, but what came out.

"Where's your med kit, and I'll take a look," Francis said. "Or I can get mine from the car."

"No. I need you to take Boone to the emergency vet." A low whine emerged from Boone's corner. I raised my voice a little. "Sorry, buddy, but you have to go ASAP, and I can't drive." When the low whine didn't subside, I said, "They have good pain meds, and it's either Francis or Anton."

Finally, Boone hushed. I wasn't sure if it was the relief of drugs or the threat of Anton, but thank goodness either way. I probably could have ridden in the car with him, but I was worried about leaving Alex alone in his current, more vulnerable condition. Emotional support for my injured hound or possession prevention for my friend. Given that Alex might do serious damage to any number of people if some vile creature took over his body, possession protection it was.

"Did you get Gabe to the police station before this mess broke out?" Anton asked. He'd disappeared into Alex's bathroom and returned carrying a small bag with a red cross on it. Apparently, he didn't need to be told where the medical supplies were.

"Yeah," Alex said. "I stayed long enough to have a look at a list of missing persons reported over the last three weeks and for him to get the license plate information for the pickup truck that was hauling you guys."

Francis hooked a leash to Boone's collar and headed to the door. I stopped him and said, "Hey, Francis, take my car. But I don't have a clue which vet you should take him to."

"I got it. I know his vet. Boone and I are old buddies."

Boone woofed in agreement, and even wagged his tail a little. So when the pair disappeared through the wrecked doorway of the office, I was feeling a little better about delegating.

"So?" Anton sounded impatient. "Any other victims on the list?" He knelt next to me and opened up the bag.

"I recognized one of the names, a coyote from north Austin. She was reported missing about two days before Patrick Twombly's disappearance. But get this: the truck was licensed to a Fred Nesmith. And I know that name. I think."

"You think? Ow." I glared at Anton. He'd ripped off Alex's T-shirt without any regard for clotting.

"What? Bleeding is good. You never know where Wembley's mouth has been." We both glanced at the air cage, but Wembley was still out. Anton lifted my arm to better inspect it, and the dull throbbing ramped back up again. "Did you even wash it?"

I gave him a wide-eyed look.

"Go wash it in the sink. Lots of soap and water." He cringed watching me ease myself off the futon, then reached down and grabbed my good arm and hauled me to my feet.

I stood there swaying for a second. When the black spots cleared, I made my way to bathroom. I could hear Alex murmuring in the background, but couldn't make out what he was saying. When I came back, the rest of Anton's medical exam was much gentler. Wild guess, Alex had threatened to rip his toenails off if he wasn't nicer to me. I couldn't imagine evil Mr. Clean making an effort for anything less.

After Anton finished dressing my arm, I asked, "How long before this thing is healed?"

After a brief beat, Anton looked at me and said, "You're asking me? You're like a lab experiment gone wrong. How should I know? Most vamps don't get blood poisoning, but if you see streaking, take some antibiotics or go see a shaman."

"A shaman?"

"To chase the bad spirits out." Anton glared. "I don't know what to tell you."

"Oh, that was a joke. Ha-ha." I shot him a nasty look. This was one dude who could suck the happy right out of any room.

"If you guys are done?" Alex looked a little less grey, but he was still really pale. "Anton, pull a basic background on this Fred Nesmith guy. Use my computer. You should at least

164

be able to get a short list of friends and family. Mallory, you probably need to eat something."

I was about to get up, when Anton held out his hand. "I got it."

He came back with a gallon jug of water and two cans of carrot juice—for me. Alex got two bottles of water. I'd have laughed, but I knew from experience that I could drink vast quantities of water, and I was starting to get the desert-dry, cotton-mouth feeling that told me I could finish off that gallon in no time.

By the time Alex had finished his two bottles of water, there was a little color in his cheeks. He hardly looked himself, but better than before.

My phone rang as Anton was grabbing a stack of papers off the printer. He snagged it off the ground where I'd dropped it a second time and chucked it at me. I let it land on the futon then retrieved it.

"Hello."

"Francis here. Boone is doing fine. Superficial burns, the vet said, but"—Francis lowered his voice—"they got after me for not bringing him in sooner. The vet said two or three days earlier would have saved him some suffering."

"What? Are you kidding me? And those burns were not superficial. I saw the guy put his...his fire hands on Boone."

Voice still low, Francis said, "Do you think he might have picked up Celia's ability to heal quickly?"

"Maybe? I guess? Either way, suck it up, say you're sorry and won't let it happen again, and get him some pain meds in case he doesn't heal them entirely. And thank you, Francis. I owe you one."

"No worries. Just wanted you to know he's okay. Do you want me to drop him at the house or with you guys at head-quarters?"

"The house." I gave him the code for the front door lock. "Thanks. Headquarters hardly feels safe right now." After I hung up, I turned to Alex in a panic. "Mandy was scheduled to work the storefront today, wasn't she? Is she okay? I didn't see her when we came in, and the front door was locked."

"She's here and should be fine shortly. You must have just missed her when you came in. There was evidence that she'd been tazed, and that shouldn't have any lasting effects on a water sprite. Anton, can you check that she's awake?"

After Anton left, I said, "I didn't think a Taser could knock a person out. And it can't be okay that she's been out this whole time." I was starting to wonder if making that air cage had fried a few of Alex's brain cells.

"Mandy's a water sprite. Electric shock is a sure way to knock a water sprite out." As he said the words, he must have had the same realization that I did, because he squeezed his eyes closed. "Not good."

"Very not good. This guy is eerily prepared."

"Freakishly prepared and equipped for exactly the type of enhanced beings he'll be encountering. Except for you. The vamp with a tolerance for caffeine."

Anton walked back in. "She wasn't awake, but I was able to revive her. I sent her home for the day. You were right; she was tazed."

"And Wembley was dosed with a massive quantity of caffeine," Alex said.

"Now that's very interesting." Anton gave me a suspicious look. "I'm guessing freak show here—sorry, *Mallory*— didn't have any issues with the caffeine."

"Ah, not exactly." I inhaled deeply. I could still detect faint traces, but the smells had mostly faded. "Alex smells like gingerbread, you smell like radishes, and I saw my Great-Aunt Lulu."

"What is she talking about?"

Alex smiled. "Synesthesia and familial hallucinations—"

I wrinkled my nose. It sounded so clinical. "I prefer ghostly sightings."

Alex chuckled. "By Mallory's standards, a nice, mild caffeine buzz."

Anton scowled at me. "I really don't see how you put up with her, Alex."

I scowled right back. "I really don't see why anyone is civil to you; you're a horrid man."

Anton looked me in the eye and then deliberately turned away. He picked up the report he'd abandoned to check on Mandy, and started to read. Just as I was trying to decide if I was happy or pissed about being snubbed by mean Mr. Clean, Anton lifted the report he'd been reading and said, "There is a connection to the Society. Fred Nesmith is John Wesley Nesmith's uncle."

"Wes Nesmith." Alex looked at me. "He's Akira's ex-husband."

"No. No way." Because I'd spoken with the man's daughter. Watched her cry. Seen the anguish in her eyes as she'd tried and failed to remember the last time she'd told her mother she loved her. "Uh-uh. No man does that to his kid."

"How about a man who hasn't had contact with his daughter in years?" Alex asked.

Anton crossed his arms. "I remember him. A weak man married to a strong woman." He looked like he'd just gotten a whiff of my vegan cheese.

Weakness wasn't much tolerated in the enhanced community, but Anton's disgust went beyond the abstract. And then a thought occurred. That reaction from a guy who was dating a hot, incredibly smart go-getter named

Rachael...who sounded an awful like Akira Mori. "Wait a second. Do you have a thing for Akira?"

"I did. My affections are currently otherwise engaged."

After several seconds, I snapped my gaping mouth closed. Mr. Clean was revealing surprising facets. I sniffed and said, "That's cool. But you're still a toad."

"And you're still a menace."

"Enough, you two," Alex said. "And we don't even know if Wes is our man. We have one piece of evidence pointing to him. That's hardly conclusive."

"And where's the motive?" I asked.

"Forget motive. What about means? He was a weak, pathetic excuse for a human being," Anton said.

I pointed at Anton. "See, now that's a problem. The guy who did this, he wasn't a little guy. He was tallish and pretty solid."

After chugging the last slug of his bottled water, Alex said, "I don't think Anton's talking about Wes's build."

"I am not. The man left his wife and child because he couldn't handle the idea of magic. Then he cut ties with his only child. Pathetically weak."

Ugh. He needed to shut up or I might actually start to like the bald toad. Or start to think of him as the not-mean Mr. Clean. Then I caught Anton glaring at me. Hm. Definitely mean. And a toad.

"So if magic is so scary," I said, "then why come back and involve himself with the Society again?"

"And how did he do it? Where's the power?" Anton asked.

"Not power. Knowledge," I said. Bradley's stupid app. It had to be. I lifted my hand to rub my pounding temple, but that made the ache in my arm turn to a fiery burn. I gritted my teeth until the pain subsided, then said, "Any chance that information would be in the mysterious source material for Bradley's app? Because last I checked, the Society doesn't issue a how-to manual during orientation on subduing and killing everyone in the Society. Not to members or their spouses."

"And yet the question remains: where's the conclusive evidence? We need to find more before we bring this to Cornelius's attention."

"Come on, Alex. The husband did it," Wembley said.

The three of us turned to Wembley, now awake and locked in a cage in the middle of Alex's office.

"I assume there's some reason that Alex risked giving himself an aneurism and bent the laws of physics to lock my butt up. And is half-naked."

"You bit Mallory." Leave it to Anton to be all sensitive and touchy-feely.

I shot Anton a nasty look. Softening my expression, I turned to Wembley and said, "But you were high on caffeine when you did it. Not yourself. Nobody blames you."

"Then why am I locked up?" Wembley didn't look particularly perturbed, just curious.

"Ah," Alex said, "that would be because I couldn't subdue you and you were trying to kill me. Or eat me. I'm not really sure."

"Aha." Wembley nodded. "That would be one reason I don't overindulge. Any ideas as to how I became intoxicated?"

"You were shot with a dart," I said, wrinkling my nose. I could still feel the sting when I thought about it. "Me too."

"Got it. Now—any chance you're going to let me out soon? It's a little cramped in here. And it looks like we need to plan a raid on a guy who's prepared for every last eventuality."

20

THE GANG'S ALL HERE

Unbending the laws of physics looked a lot easier than bending them. Without breaking a sweat, Alex dissolved the bars of Wembley's cage. As they disappeared, a puff of air brushed my cheek.

"That is so incredibly cool. Next time I ask you what kind of magic wizards can do, Alex, this is the stuff I'm talking about." Then I walked up to Wembley and gave him a bear hug.

"Forgive me?" he whispered in my ear.

"Not even a little bit." I squeezed him tighter. "There's nothing to forgive."

When he let me go, he lifted my hand and examined the bandage. "I suppose now we get to find out exactly how fast you heal."

"That is a bonus. And it won't keep me and Tangwystl out of the fight. We've got a name, and that should help us find a place."

"Working on it," Alex called from his desk. He'd pulled on a navy T-shirt and was bent over his laptop, looking much more chipper now that we had a viable lead. He could talk about needing more evidence, but the guy looked pretty energized by the prospect of confronting the as-yet-to-be-determined-guilty Wes Sherwood.

"Maybe he has a partner." I was trying to think how pathetic, weak human Wes could be whooping up a bunch on supercharged enhanced people. "Great planning only takes you so far."

"What about your parasite idea?" Wembley asked. "Think about it. You've got a demigod, a nine-tailed kitsune, and a phoenix. If he could take something from them..."

I snapped my fingers. "A coyote. Alex, didn't you say one had gone missing?"

"More than a week ago. I recognized the name on the missing persons list that Ruiz put together."

"Is there any way that a human can steal enhanced talents? Because if Wes could do that, and he grabbed a coyote—someone with excellent illusion and persuasion skills but not much in the way of offensive magic—then he might have started with more vulnerable targets and worked his way up."

Alex and Anton shared a look. I just about yelled. I wasn't sure what I'd holler, but hollering seemed like a great idea. They knew something and had been hoarding that information like miserly little magical Scrooges.

"Calm down, crazy woman," Anton said.

No, he didn't.

"You're an idiot," Alex said to Anton, shaking his head. "You need to thank the stars that the lovely Rachael doesn't mind dating down."

Which made me want to giggle, because I thought it pretty routinely. So satisfying to hear Alex said it out loud.

Wembley nudged me, and when I looked, he said quietly, "Your eyes were bleeding."

"Ah." I could feel my face flush. I gritted my teeth then turned to Alex and Anton and said, "What are you guys hiding?"

"Not hiding, just didn't think it was relevant until now. Cornelius has been doing some research on that necklace we recovered last week. He suspects the pendant was one of several jewels that made up the original necklace. This particular piece has an unusual history."

Finding that necklace felt like a lifetime ago. Or at least a whole almost-date and a kidnapping ago. "So what's the story on the necklace? Something more disgusting than sucking out the life juice of a golem?"

"No confirmation," Alex said, "but given the properties of the stone, Cornelius suspects it's a part of a famous necklace that belonged to a notorious nineteenth century woman of ill repute."

"Ah." A faint look of disgust crossed Wembley's face. "I don't suppose he was speaking of a Georgian amethyst necklace? Belonging to Bethia Belleau?"

"One and the same," Alex said. "I'm not familiar with her."

"You were still in Europe at the time. I was already stateside." Wembley dropped down onto Alex's futon. If I didn't know my ex-berserker Viking roomie better, I'd say he looked squeamish. "She was mistress to the powerful, the wealthy, and the beautiful of the nineteenth century. And, quite famously among the enhanced, a succubus."

"Uh, does that mean what I think it means? Sucking life juice out of men while having sex with them?" I asked.

"Correct. A beautifully terrible way to pass, I hear," Anton said with a twitchy shiver.

I tried not to revel in Anton's discomfort—but then I remembered why I disliked the man so much, and reveled away. It was thoroughly satisfying to see him so discom-bobulated.

Bethia's jewelry, that was what we needed to be discussing. "So her necklace retained some of her abilities? That's batty." But then there was the dead golem guy who'd had his golem battery drained, quite possibly by one of the stones from Bethia's necklace. "Or maybe there's some logical explanation?"

"Even if the necklace has some power," Wembley said, "that should have diminished or vanished when it was disassembled."

"And who takes apart a piece of history like that?" I glared back at Anton when he gave me a dirty look. "Watch it, buddy. We might discover my bleeding eyes do something nifty and weird. I am a freak show, after all, or wait—a science experiment gone wrong? Isn't that what you called me?"

"A comment I'm sure Anton thoroughly regrets," Alex said from his desk. "And you can stop squabbling, because I've got an address."

"Wait, what? For evil, power-stealing Wes?" I hustled to peer over his shoulder, only to find a chat window open with Bradley. "Wow. I don't even get to IM with Bradley. I might be feeling inferior right now as a ninja-sleuth. Isn't that outside of town, down south? We should maybe load up and get a move on."

Anton looked around the small group. "Bad idea. You're injured, Alex is one solid shove away from toppling, and Wembley's coming off an epic high."

I eyed Alex and decided Anton was overreacting. "I don't know, Alex. What do you think? You think our baddie is gonna hang out and wait for us to recover before he hauls booty to Mexico? Or wherever the enhanced community goes to hide out?"

"Australia," Wembley said, "and I'm recovered enough to fight."

"Anton," Alex said, "gather up a few fire extinguishers."

Once Anton had left, Alex retrieved his sword from a cabinet.

I thought Alex's sword was always on hand, but invisible. Now I knew he had a physical place to store it, and it didn't live in the ether surrounding him. But I still believed that whole ether thing was possible after seeing him mind-bend air into a solid.

And speaking of hidden talents... "If Wes is stealing enhancements, then fire, illusion, and persuasion are all on the table. But what exactly did he gain from Akira and Patrick-Elvis?"

Alex grabbed a page off the wireless printer in the corner of the office. "With Patrick, he gains the subtle ability to generate adoration, but a little more immediate and handier is the ability to alter his appearance."

I rubbed my forehead. "You've got to be kidding me. Just when I can finally see his face in my memories. I'm guessing that was persuasion and illusion, and it doesn't work now that I know who he is."

Alex looked up from his phone and nodded, as Anton returned with two fire extinguishers.

Anton lifted the two canisters. "Can't you do this with magic?"

Given Alex's physics-defying manipulation of the properties of air, my money was on him in a standoff against Wes's flames. Which was seriously cool. Then I remembered how wiped he'd been. "Except that would be a bad idea when a container of chemicals can do it just as well."

I glared at Anton, willing him to shut his mouth when it looked like he'd comment. The jerk almost made ripping a throat open palatable. Blech. If I could gargle with bleach after.

"To answer your question about Akira's powers, Mallory," Wembley said, "Wes might be able to take the form of a fox, but I doubt he has gained her psychic abilities—or, if he has, that he can control them." He shrugged. "Supposition, but that's my best guess."

Flames, a sneaky-fast fox form, a sword— "Oh! Hey, guys, I have some good news. Our guy sucks with a sword. So if we can keep the fire and illusion and persuasion and shape-shifting under control, we can totally kick this guy's butt."

"Was that supposed to be motivational?" Wembley asked.

"Yes?"

Alex winked at me—he *winked*. Or I imagined it, because that was just too weird for words. "Let's go. Star is meeting us there."

Of course—Star was in Buda, right around the corner from our bad guy's hideout. Now *that* bit of news was motivational.

21

CHARGE!

Twenty minutes later, crouched behind my Grand Cherokee with Wembley's revolver clenched in my hand, I was starting to doubt our impulsive charge. Not like we'd had much choice. Wes had known we were onto him, and he would almost definitely have fled, regardless of what Anton said.

So here we were, Star and I as decoys, sitting in his driveway, the guys sneaking around like thieves, and Wes holed up with Patrick-Elvis and Akira hostage.

A fireball landed at my feet and poofed out almost immediately, leaving nothing but charred grass in its wake. Lord love that air-manipulating, overprotective partner of mine.

Except he was supposed to be sneaking around the north side of the property while Wembley took the south. Anton got the fun job of trespassing on the neighbor's property to circle the perimeter of the acreage and come up the back.

I crawled further behind my Jeep and looked over at Star. "Glad you could meet us."

Her pale complexion had a rosy glow, and her elfin features were more animated than I'd ever seen before. "No worries. This is the part I missed."

"You missed standoffs with maniacal nut jobs holding hostages?" And she'd seemed almost sane before today.

"Absolutely." She lifted her 9mm in a cheery salute. "I'll go this time. You're making Alex nervous, and he needs to be focused on a stealthy entry."

I nodded. If she wanted to have fireballs lobbed at her— okay. I hefted the fire extinguisher stashed by the Jeep's tire. "It's a shame you don't have a fireproof cloak, or some kind of shield."

"I think I have something in storage, but we were on a tight timeline." She fired a round at the door.

I shook my head. "How exactly are we sure that we're not hitting a hostage?"

"We're not *certain*, but odds are they're passed out and locked up." She fired another shot. "Incoming."

I eyed the ball of flames, calculated a rough trajectory, figured he'd hit the hood or short of it, and readied the fire extinguisher. I popped up and flinched at the sound of Star's cover fire. But then one quick blast and the would-be fire in front of the car was out.

"I'm still thinking hiding behind a car with a big ol' gas tank attached to it isn't the brightest idea when we're dealing with fireballs."

"Think again. The problem with stealing someone else's magic is that it takes time, discipline, and practice to master using it."

"I was wondering about his terrible aim, and these fire-balls do seem to be more lobbed than shot. My turn?" I wrinkled my nose.

"I'll go again. Ready?" When I nodded, she came out shooting.

Except this time, the door was firmly closed and there was no return volley.

"Maybe you got him?"

Star checked her clip, counted the rounds, and shook her head. "No. I think the guys are in. Come on." She opened the driver's-side door and motioned for me to crawl over to the passenger side.

As I crawled, I made an awesome target. Sure, Star had me covered and the front door was still firmly shut—but there were a few windows on the front of the house. I watched for a twitch of the curtains, but they remained closed as I crawled over the center console. Once Star was in the driver's seat, I asked, "How long do you think we have until the neighbors call the cops?"

"What neighbors? The property Anton was supposed to skirt is a hunting cabin and shouldn't be occupied, and no one lives on the other side. Besides, this is the country."

That seemed awfully optimistic, but my concern about potential police interference faded as she drove straight up the drive toward the front door. "You do know we get easier to hit as we get closer, right?"

Star waved a hand, like it was no concern.

That might have reassured me more if it hadn't been the hand holding her gun. I ducked as the barrel moved in my direction. I decided that maybe silence was the best option, and hunkered down as low as I could.

Star passed by the front door without sparking even a twitch of the curtains, and then round to the back—where the back door stood wide open.

"Come on," Star said as she got out of the car.

I dropped Wembley's revolver into the glovebox and

grabbed Tangwystl. "Sure thing, but promise me if I get shot it won't be friendly fire."

A disturbing silence followed.

I took a deep breath, drew Tangwystl, and followed Star into the house. Today might be the day I discovered exactly what bullets would do to me. Lucky me.

"Sharp as you like, Tangwystl," I whispered to my sword as I walked into Wes's kitchen.

Her squee of delight made me wince.

When I opened my eyes, I saw that Star and I weren't alone in the kitchen. Wes stood directly to Star's right.

I lunged, hoping I was fast enough to reach him before he hurt Star.

As he sidestepped and spun, he said, "Watch it, freak show."

And I almost tripped over my own feet. Only Anton called me freak show.

"Hold, Mallory," Star said. "It's an illusion. That's Anton."

I caught myself before I fell, probably on top of Tangwystl. "What the heck is going on?" I stage-whispered. But before Anton even said a word, the image of Wes melted away and there was mean Mr. Clean. "Illusion—got it."

And as my brain tried to untangle the improbable from the impossible, I heard the clash of blades.

Star was a step ahead of me, so I trailed behind her as she left the kitchen and moved deeper into the house.

We entered a dark dining room filled with tables. I blinked into the dimness and squinted. Not tables. Stretchers. "Oh, no."

Four stretchers. Two were empty but two had bundles atop them. Except they wouldn't be bundles—would they? My mind drifted to the word I wanted so much to avoid:

corpses. And then Anton disappeared, leaving Star and me to cope with whatever was atop those stretchers.

Light flared as Star flipped the switch, and I was briefly blinded by the brightness.

Star's touch on my arm made me jump. "Jeez, woman. Don't touch the crazy wounded lady with the sharp sword."

"You're not crazy." Star moved closer to one of the stretchers as she spoke. Given her behavior today, I wasn't feeling particularly reassured by her comment.

I reminded myself that I didn't know Patrick-Elvis, not really. And Akira was a stranger to me. Then I trailed behind Star, my gaze shifting between the two points of egress and the entirely-too-still bundles that had been revealed as sheet-covered people.

We reached Patrick-Elvis first. He wasn't restrained. His body was so pale, so still that I was uncertain if he was dead or unconscious. But then I saw his hands, one atop the other, arranged over his stomach, and I flashed back to the image of the man in Star's mortuary.

Star reached out and grasped his wrist between her thumb and two fingers. "He has a pulse, a faint pulse." She moved a few feet more to the next stretcher and then said, "Akira as well."

And I felt whatever had held me upright to that point melt away as relief crashed through me.

Suddenly, Star was by my side and grasping my good arm in a firm grip. "Are you okay?"

"Yep. All good."

"Well, that's one of us, then." She didn't look nearly as relieved as I felt. She pointed.

I followed her finger to Patrick-Elvis's throat—where a purple gemstone nestled in the hollow below his Adam's apple.

I might have lacked the ability to perceive magic in the past, but there was no mistaking the flicker and throb of the stone as it sucked magic away from Patrick-Elvis.

I took a step closer, and Star said, "Don't touch." She pointed to an identical stone placed in the hollow of Akira's throat.

"Yeah, I got that. Is it safe to leave them—like this, with these parasite stones still in place—for a little while?" I was worried about the rest of the team. Star and I had only been in the living room a minute, a minute and a half, but the sounds of fighting had gotten louder. Alex, Wembley, and Anton should have easily taken down a single man.

"I need to stay and figure out a way to detach the stones without doing damage to the hosts." Star looked grim, which meant Patrick-Elvis and Akira were far from safe. "But you can't help me."

"If Wes has a partner—"

"Go." Star had already dismissed me and was focusing all of her considerable energy and talent on Patrick-Elvis.

I spun around and jogged down a hall toward the sounds of scuffling. Tangwystl ready, I turned the corner and stepped into a large living room—and rocked back on my heels.

Wembley had a death grip on a squirming, oversized fox. But that wasn't nearly as surprising as the wrestling match taking place in the center of the room.

Alex had abandoned his sword and was grappling with Anton. Both looked bruised, bloody, and determined to win.

I turned back to Wembley, who appeared to be strangling the fox. "What are you doing?"

The fox spat and hissed and scrabbled with its back legs, ripping furrows in Wembley's legs.

"Trying to get this nasty bit of fur to release the glamor

he placed on Anton." He punctuated his statement with a hard shake.

I tried to walk in the room, but couldn't begin to see a path past the two men trying to pound each other to a bloody pulp. "Wembley, you've got to stop them."

Alex kicked Anton in the junk and said, "Please. I can't pull another air cage yet." He wiped blood and spit from his mouth. But his reprieve only lasted a moment; Anton was already bouncing back.

"Why isn't he just flaming them both?" I hollered across the room at Wembley.

"Don't think he can as a fox." Wembley cursed. "Of course, that means that I also need him human to remove the glamor. Thanks, doll."

Since the hint I'd given him had been completely accidental, I didn't have a good response. I rubbed my sword's hilt and whispered, "I need a dull blade, Tangwystl."

But no bloods. No stabby, no bloods.

"Blood," I said automatically, correcting her speech. "No blood. I know, just give me a dull edge, please."

She sniffed, and I saw the impossible razor's edge of the sword melt away.

I hadn't a clue what I could do that Alex couldn't, but I couldn't stand by and watch— Uh-oh. Wembley had just chucked the red ball of fox fur he'd been strangling against a wall.

I felt bad for the fox, until it crumpled in a heap of very human arms and legs. Wes staggered to his feet, I thought in a disoriented stupor.

And I kept thinking that until Anton smashed a fist into Alex's face and turned straight to me with a blazing look of hatred.

"Wembley," I called as I lifted my blunt sword and

hoped with all my heart that Anton wasn't nearly as strong as he looked.

He was, though. I knew he was.

And he was coming.

A shriek pierced my skull as Anton attacked.

Then everything was silent. Still. Dark.

It was the smell that clued me in. I could smell blood and sweat. Mostly the blood, which my stomach did not appreciate. I shoved hard at the mountain of muscle that was on top of me. And Anton rolled off me without resisting. "Great. I've killed the jerk."

"I'm not dead, freak show," Anton said as he stood up.

"You're you," I said. Which made about as much sense to me as it did to the very confused Anton.

He offered me a hand up.

I snagged Tangwystl from the floor and then accepted his hand. When I was on my feet, I saw a very dead Wes Sheffield. Wembley stood over his body with a curiously blank expression on his face.

"What just happened?" I asked.

Anton looked at Wembley, the body, Alex, and then me. "A lot of magic."

Which told me exactly nothing. I turned to ask Alex to explain, but the words wouldn't come. Because Alex wasn't okay.

22

A MAGICAL KILL

Alex collapsed back against the far wall of the living room, avoiding my gaze. He looked drained, disgusted, tired...devastated. Almost as bad as the time he'd been possessed.

Which made no sense. Bad guy dead—that was a win for us. Not the result we might have hoped for, but in the land of emergency response cases and chasing guys who were going to be executed for their crimes anyway...I figured that would hardly be a tragedy.

"I don't understand—"

"Hey!" Star called from across the house. "What just happened?" Her voice got louder as she got closer. She walked into the room and seemed to size everything up in the blink of an eye. She wrapped an arm around my shoulders and turned me toward the exit. "Let's go. You can help me with Patrick and Akira. They're awake."

"But..." I couldn't leave Alex. Not looking the way he did. Feeling the way he did.

Star's arm tightened around me, and very quietly, very clearly, she said, "Trust me, he doesn't want you here now."

Once we arrived in the dining room, there was no time for questions. I met Akira, who was communicative and waking with no assistance, and was reintroduced to Patrick-Elvis, who was much weaker.

After explaining where they were and what had happened, Star and I escorted them to my Jeep, and the four of us left.

I protested, but Star assured me the rest of the team would be picked up shortly, and she needed my help getting Akira and Patrick home.

Star drove, and I kept Patrick company in the back seat. While Akira spoke with her daughter and assured her she was completely fine, Patrick-Elvis napped on and off. The drive seemed to last an eternity. I had so many questions, but could hardly discuss them with Akira and Patrick-Elvis in the car. They'd been through enough already.

Although—I glanced at Patrick-Elvis—he seemed to be recovering very quickly. Much like Alex after his air cage exploit.

"He drugged me," Patrick-Elvis said.

"I'm sorry?"

"If you were wondering how he got the jump on me. He knocked on my door, asked for an autograph, and tranquilized me. I'm not sure how; I don't remember. But I'm as susceptible to narcotics as the original version was, and since the original was human—there you have it."

I sighed. "Sheffield was freakishly well informed regarding the weaknesses of his targets. I'm sure the Society will be investigating the source of that information."

Patrick-Elvis nodded.

"We went to your show. At Tiaras."

"I'm sorry you didn't get to see the show. Next time." He flashed me the smile I remembered so well from the police station. The one that more than hinted at Patrick's origins. Patrick. Not Patrick-Elvis. Because the man sitting next to me wasn't the King. He was his own man, and his name was Patrick Twombly.

Star was pulling off the freeway, when I realized I might not have another chance to ask Akira about her message.

After she'd ended her call with her daughter, she'd ridden silently, watching the world pass by outside the car window. I could only imagine how terrifying her experience had been.

"Akira?" I said softly.

She looked over her shoulder, an expectant look on her face.

"We got your message, but we didn't understand it. What were the images supposed to represent?"

"I was concerned they would create confusion, but I had only a split second before I lost consciousness to imprint them upon the room. All three images were the same message. I was trying to convey the identity of my attacker."

The image of the man, that I understood. Her daughter was also clear in retrospect, since our bad guy was her father. But..."I don't understand the image of the cell phone."

Akira shook her head. "He dropped his phone, and it was the last thing I saw before I lost consciousness. The background image was an old family photo: Wes, Michelle, and me."

"Ah, we just saw the phone with a blank screen. And the image of Wes that you sent came across as a faceless man."

"He must have interfered with the psychic imprint." A deep crease formed between her eyes. "I'm not sure how he could have done that. You know he was fully human at one time."

"I do." Star pulled into the Society headquarters parking lot, and I said, "Cornelius should be able to answer some of your questions—after you see your daughter."

Cornelius and Michelle were both waiting in the parking lot. The look on Michelle's face made me go all teary. And once Akira saw her daughter, she put aside questions about her ex.

I was glad to escape any long goodbyes when Star asked if I was ready to go home.

Cornelius didn't even make a fuss about debriefing or paperwork. There was a notable lack fuss, actually.

As soon as we pulled out of the parking lot, Star said, "There's something you need to know...I couldn't discuss it with others in the car." She paused, and when she spoke again, the words came slowly, as if drug from her. "There's a difference between killing with a sword and killing with magic."

I sat up straighter as tension pulsed through my body. "Are you telling me Alex is in trouble with the Society?"

"No, nothing like that. Wes was an execution waiting to happen. Occasionally, a mundane gets a taste of magic and they try to make the transformation—but it doesn't take. That can leave psychological scars." Star tucked a stray piece of bright blonde hair behind her ear. "He was basically a failed witch: aware of the power but unable to touch it or harness it. You do understand that witches are made, not born?"

I nodded. "Alex said it begins with study."

"That's right. But you can study the entirety of your life and never become a witch. The magic has to take a liking to you. It becomes a part of you, changes you, and then you're transformed. That transformation eluded Wes Sheffield, and he chased it in ways I'm not entirely sure I understand."

She grew still, driving down the last few streets in silence. Only when she'd pulled into my driveway did she speak again. "Alex won't have any difficulties with the Society. It's a question of the problems he's created for himself. Killing with a sword might weigh on a man's conscience, but killing with magic stains a man's soul."

"That makes no sense at all. What does the method have to do with anything?"

"It simply does; I can't explain why. I've never killed with magic before." She took the keys from the ignition and handed them to me. "He must have felt death was imminent, or he wouldn't have done it."

No. That much I knew she had wrong. He'd done it to save me. Sheffield had pitted Anton against Alex, effectively tying his hands because he wouldn't seriously harm his friend. And when Anton had turned on me, Alex must have thought the only solution was to take out Sheffield. There hadn't been time to retrieve his sword, to stop Sheffield using any physical means.

"How did you know?" I asked. "When you came in the room, you knew exactly what had happened."

"There was only one person in the room who could have caused Wes Sheffield's injuries. Alex can manipulate air into a liquid or solid. Pulverizing a heart is simple enough in comparison." Star looked at me closely. "You don't look so good."

"Yeah, I don't feel so good." But it wasn't the blood or the nature of Sheffield's injuries that made me cringe.

Alex was a swordsman first and a wizard second. He'd openly admitted to acting as the Society's executioner on more than one occasion. But he'd crossed the line, from killing by the sword to killing with magic, because of me. Because I'd been in trouble.

Even if I didn't fully understand, I knew enough for my stomach to churn.

"My ride's here," Star said, pointing to Anton's Escalade pulling up to the curb.

Wembley hopped out, looking mostly recovered.

"Thanks, Star," I gave her a weak smile. "I hope you get a massive bonus for this."

"No. This one's on the house." She leaned across the center console and gave me a hug.

EPILOGUE

Two days and not a peep from Alex. I'd been tempted to text him, but Wembley said he was rough and needed a few days of recovery time.

Personally, if he was that rough, I thought he should have a friend nearby. Someone should be making sure he didn't run into trouble with spiritual hitchhikers, because the last thing Alex needed right now was to be possessed or harassed by demons.

I'd poked at Wembley, and he'd swung by a few times to make sure everything was going okay, and he swore Alex was neither possessed or harassed by demons and that he was sleeping and eating well.

The doorbell rang. I jumped to my feet and hollered, "Got it!"

I swung open the door to find Detective Ruiz standing on my doorstep. He was holding a fall bouquet full of oranges and reds and yellows.

He handed the flowers to me and said, "Hi."

Maybe it was because I'd been thinking of Alex when the doorbell sounded, or because I'd been so worried about him these last few days, but when I opened the door, I'd expected it to be him.

After a brief hesitation, wherein my brain reconciled what I'd expected to see with what was in front of my eyes, I took the flowers. "Thank you. They're gorgeous."

Simple enough to say, because they were. But then the significance of him appearing on my doorstep slowly sank in, and I grinned at him. "Would you like to come inside?"

"No, thanks. I can't stay. I just wanted to drop by and let you know that Sofia Kontos, your phoenix, is awake. Since the hospital had no idea why she was unconscious for several days, they wanted to hold her. But she declined and released herself against her doctor's recommendation."

First flowers and now this. The day was looking brighter by the moment. Now if only I'd hear from Alex... My manners kicked in, and I said, "Thank you so much for letting me know. I debriefed with Cornelius yesterday. He told me that the stones are parasitic in nature, and, once removed, the host can begin recovering and recharging his or her magical battery, so to speak. As long as the stone is removed before the host becomes critically damaged." I couldn't resist the pull of the bouquet. I stopped to smell the flowers, burying my nose in them. "Oh, I got a call from Patrick yesterday. He's doing a lot better and said that Akira was practically back to normal."

I didn't mention the other things I'd learned in my debrief. That the Society was on alert for the source materials used to create Bradley's app, because the book hadn't been in Wes's possession. That Cornelius had refused to fully immunize Bradley against prosecution for future damages stemming from his unintentional dissemination of top-secret Society info. That Wes must have learned how to harvest the stolen magic stored in the stones from someone.

There weren't exactly books on the procedure—not so far as Cornelius knew. And finally, that the young coyote woman, Wes Sheffield's first victim, hadn't been found alive.

None of that information was secret, not now that Gabe was a Society insider. I wasn't ready. I was prepared to celebrate the wins of my most recent adventure, but ill prepared for anything else at this point. In a few days...but not now.

"That's great news."

I blinked at him in confusion, trying to find way back to the piece of good news I had verbalized. "Oh, Patrick and Akira, yes, definitely."

Gabe grasped the doorframe with his right hand and leaned forward a few inches. "Is there any chance that you'd be interested in dinner?"

It took me a second to switch gears from adventure fallout to romance. But at least I didn't have to think about whether it was a *date* date. When a guy brings you flowers and asks you out to dinner, there's not much room for interpretation. And it felt nice. More than nice.

I gave him a brilliant smile. "Yes, I'd love that."

"Tomorrow night, eight o'clock? I'll pick you up?"

I nodded, with what was likely a goofy grin plastered to my face. "Perfect."

And then he leaned forward and kissed me.

Nothing X-rated, or even R, for that matter. Just a gentle, brief pressure of lips. More a precursor to a kiss than the real thing.

So it wasn't shocking that I didn't see fireworks or feel the earth move. But it was nice. Nice to feel wanted. Nice to be appreciated as a woman. Nice to be seen as desirable and not something strange, unique, or broken.

It was nice, right up until he stepped back, and I saw Alex's Juke roll up next to my curb. Not that Alex had seen the innocent kiss. I was sure he hadn't. But that wasn't the point. I felt guilty. For innocently kissing a man who'd just asked my very single self out on a date.

Why would I feel guilty?

"I'll see you tomorrow evening," Gabe said as he turned away.

The two men passed on the path leading up to my house. And as they briefly stood next to each other, it was tall, lanky Alex who drew my eye. Alex who tugged at my heart.

And that was why I felt guilty.

Alex eyed the flowers I held, and glanced over his shoulder at Gabe's retreating car. "That doesn't look like a get-well bouquet."

"No, he asked me out on a date." I didn't look closely at Alex as I spoke, because I didn't want to see his reaction. I just didn't want to lie or hide the truth. "Come inside?" I opened the door wider.

He hesitated just a fraction of a second and then strolled by me. As I shut the door after him, he said, "I thought you'd want to hear the good news in person."

He headed straight for the kitchen.

Since I felt like a little caffeine or maybe a midday scotch, that was okay with me. And I had flowers to deal with.

I set the flowers on the counter and retrieved a pair of scissors. I pointed up at a cabinet above my head and said, "Do you mind? There's a clear vase up there that should work for these."

Wordlessly, he retrieved the vase.

I started to trim the flowers as he filled the vase with water. "What's this good news?"

He set the vase down on the counter to my right. "Boone is officially yours."

I dropped the flowers into the vase and then turned to look at him. I leaned back against the counter as a smile stretched across my face. "How in the world did you manage that?"

He shrugged. "Without you, no one can communicate with him. Cornelius's thoughts were along the lines of: how could the Society allow such a well-trained, unique animal to go to waste?"

"And he didn't need any nudging to reach that conclusion? *Right*. Thank you."

"No problem. Are you planning to attend Marisol's funeral?"

Marisol. That was the young coyote woman's name. "Yes. Of course." My eyes burned, but I wasn't ready to cry. I turned back to my flowers and inhaled. The pretty scent pushed away the burn of tears.

I looked at him—really looked—and could see that he was ragged around the edges. While I'd been focusing on the win, I wasn't so sure Alex had done the same. We'd recovered three of Sheffield's four victims, but if I knew Alex, it would be the failure that stuck.

And that wasn't even touching the whole soul-staining magical death issue.

I turned to him and wrapped my arms around him. He stood very still and let me hug him, but didn't reciprocate.

So I hugged him tighter. And—eventually—he hugged me back.

As I stood in the circle of his arms, my heart hurt for him.

He leaned down and whispered in my ear, "I think your mother is calling."

I stepped back. "What?"

"Your phone's ringing, and it sounds like your mom's ringtone."

"Nuts."

He grinned then went to fetch my phone. "You've been avoiding her, haven't you?"

"Wouldn't you if you'd lost some obscene amount of weight in an impossibly short amount of time?" I stared at the phone he was offering me until it stopped ringing, then I took it. Reluctantly.

"It's been over a month. She'll just think you've been dieting." Alex eyed me critically then ducked his head until he caught my eye. "It's not just that, is it?"

"Ugh." I crossed my arms and squished up my face. I hated to even say the words out loud. "I think she and Wembley have been dating."

Alex chuckled, the sound beginning low in his chest and rolling out in mellow, deep tones. And *that* made my heart hurt a little less.

THE END

BONUS CONTENT

Sign up for my newsletter to receive release announcements, bonus materials, and a sampling of my different series. Sign up at http://eepurl.com/b9IH5v

ABOUT THE AUTHOR

Cate Lawley is the pen name for Kate Baray's sweet romances and cozy mysteries, including The Goode Witch Matchmaker and Vegan Vamp series. When she's not tapping away at her keyboard or in deep contemplation of her next fanciful writing project, she's sweeping up hairy dust bunnies and watching British mysteries with her pointers and hounds.

Cate also writes urban and paranormal fantasy as Kate Baray and thrillers as K.D. Baray.

For more information:
www.catelawley.com
www.facebook.com/katebaray
www.twitter.com/katebarayauthor